C OME-B Y-C HANCE
BRIDES OF 1885

BOOK TWO

Coral

by
JULIET JAMES

dedicated to all those who need the strength to let go

1

CORAL MELLORS' MOTHERLY INSTINCTS WARNED HER, one full minute before it began.

She gathered her Willie up into her arms, held him close and looked out through the curtains at the Kansas City street.

Dread.

That's what she felt. A sense of doom, the like of which she had never felt before. Not when she had met her husband. Not when she had married him. Not even on those nights he had come home from the gambling house, roaring and flaming, blaming Coral for all his bad luck, then taking it all out on her with his fists.

He was a horrible man, to be sure, but he had been gone from her life for two years now. Sam Mellors had been run out of town after one bad horse-trade too many. For all Coral knew, he was dead. But dead or alive, he was never expected to return. Still, *never* is a long time, as Coral was about to find out.

"Put the child down and stop mollycoddling him," slurred Coral's mother-in-law. It was only late morning, but the woman was three parts through her first bottle of the day. When sober, she was well spoken, pleasant and animated. Unfortunately, she was rarely sober.

"Please, Verna! I've asked you not to call him that. You know he's sensitive."

"The child is useless, that's what he is — just like his father, and his father's father before him. And the sooner you accept it, the easier it will be for you. There was never a Mellors worth marrying, and I'm sorry, Coral, but you made that mistake just as I did." Verna Mellors took another swig from her bottle and slumped back in the wicker chair, her legs all spread out, her eyes rolling halfway back in her head.

"Horsie!" cried the almost three-year-old Willie, his eyes lighting up as he watched through the window. There was nothing in the world that young Willie Mellors loved quite so much as the sight and sound of a horse, and this one was headed right for his house.

In that moment, Coral found out the cause of her dread feeling, or at least the beginnings of it — Sam Mellors was back, riding hard for his family home, a desperate man on a desperate mission. He wheeled the galloping horse around hard, a cloud of thick dust flying up in his wake, and turned into the lane that led to the back of his mother's house. And in that instant, Coral saw clearly, by the grimness of his face, that the man had not changed his ways — and trouble was sure to soon follow.

Young Roy Black was feeling old.

He had stayed inside this morning instead of going out and helping his brothers. And while he knew it was wrong, he just could not drag his behind out of bed, not even to go to the kitchen and eat.

Yes, Roy Black felt mighty tired, and mighty old into the bargain.

It was all he could manage to lie in the darkened room and think about what might be wrong.

Sure, he was barely twenty-five, but many of the *younger* men from around Come-By-Chance — most of the good men at least — had recently found themselves wonderful brides.

All three Wilkinson boys were younger than Roy for a start, and each of them had married fine women this past year — in fact two of the three were already fathers. Roy's friend Henry Miller had married well too, and not only was *he* barely twenty, but his wife Rose had come to him with a ready-made family, four children in total, and they were keen to add to that number just as soon as they could!

Then there was young Gilbert Milligan, who had come back from the big city to run his parents' store in town. Well, before you could say *The-Church-Is-On-Fire*, Gilbert had not only saved the whole town, but had got himself hitched to Emmy-Lou Waters, whose father was now about to build the first ever Come-By-Chance bank — and Gilbert would run it of course.

It had seemed, briefly, that Roy had been in with a chance at marrying Rose, and he had liked the idea, had liked the idea very much. But Henry had come back to town, and he and Rose were happy together, so Roy was most happy for them both.

Then, not so long after, Roy's friend and mentor Wally Davis — Wally had become more like a father than a friend, really — had suggested that Roy would make the best husband for Opal Bye when she came into town just last month. She was a striking young woman indeed, with many fine qualities, and Roy would have been tickled pink to marry her. But Opal, too, had been destined to marry another, the good Sheriff Johnson — and while Roy was happy for all these fine men, he was beginning to wonder if ever he would get his own turn at becoming a family man.

Yes, without a wife and family, and stuck here on the

farm with all these dang crops, Roy's life felt empty at best. At least when they had run cattle he had been on a horse much of the time, but farming felt all wrong to him, and he was beginning to wonder what use he was to the world.

Roy scolded himself for thinking this way, and determined to do something about it. Dragging himself from his bed seemed like a good start, so he got up, pulled on his britches, washed his face with cool water, and forced himself to go to the kitchen.

He needed to drag himself up out of this mood, and lying around in his bed wouldn't do it. It was already halfway through the morning, after all. With both parents now gone, and Roy being the eldest, he felt a great responsibility to his brothers — and he was setting a bad example, lying around while they did all the work. And worse, today was not the first time he'd done it.

He began to fry up a meal, but even the rich smell of sizzling bacon didn't lift him the way that it used to. Then, before he was done cooking, his brothers came in from their work, and the youngest, Milt, said, "Feelin' better, Roy? Throw some more bacon in there, let's all have some."

Ordinarily, Roy would have been happy to cook up extra for his brothers, but today, something about Milt's words just stuck in his craw. "Cook it yourself, I ain't your maidservant."

"Maidservant?" said Marty sharply. He was twenty, a year older than Milt, and had always been quick to get riled up. "Beggin' your pardon, King Roy, but we's been workin' all mornin' while you lay about in bed surveyin' your kingdom."

Roy felt his hands form into fists, but before he could make a move, their other brother Archie stepped between Roy and Marty, saying, "Calm down, boys, no need to fight. I'll fry up the bacon, and we'll all have a talk and get to the bottom o' things."

"He's just gone bone lazy, that's the bottom of things!" said Marty.

"Leave him be, Marty," said Milt. "He's missin' Ma is all, ain't it, Roy? Ain't it? I miss her too!"

Roy knew he'd been lazy, knew it wasn't his brothers' fault how he felt, but he knew there was more to it than just missing his Ma as well. "I'm sorry, boys," he said. "I don't know what's wrong with me. I miss Ma, but we all do — it ain't just that. And I gotta admit the truth, I ain't sick — not proper sick anyways. But I can't seem to get movin' these mornin's, I just can't."

At twenty-three, Archie was the second eldest, and had really come into his own since the death of their Pa. Before then, all four boys had been mostly scared to speak up or do anything excepting whatever their Pa told them to, the man's way always having been to hit first and ask questions later.

The boys had been somewhat sad at his death, of course, but in truth, there had been mixed feelings — for Horace Black had always been a cruel man, not just to the boys, but to their Ma too, and they had all loved their Ma dearly.

"You know, Roy," said Archie as he threw some more bacon into the pan and breathed in the delicious smell of it, "I been thinkin'. You maybe just need a break from the farm for a spell. It's been a difficult couple o' years, and you done a dang fine job o' holding the family together. You done right by us all, Roy, and you should be proud. And we got the farm runnin' smoother'n a cougar's pelt now. So I been thinkin', maybe you could go travelin' about some, the way ol' Wally done when *he* was a young fella. Might even find one o' them big nuggets o' gold like he did."

Wally Davis had become like a father to the boys since their Pa died, which some people found strange, seeing as how Horace had died while in the act of trying to kill Wally. But old Wally had known Horace Black was a plain evil man, and that his boys deserved a chance — and he had very quickly decided to help them become the very best men they could be.

"Maybe you're right, Arch," said Roy. He did not make mention of how tired and old he was feeling, or even that he was upset at missing out on every bride that had come to the town, while the young woman he himself had written to had never written him back but the once. But he heard the sense in Archie's words, and decided it wouldn't hurt to change his surroundings a while. "Thanks, Arch. And sorry, boys, for my recent bad temper. I'll mosey on over to see Wally and have a talk about it all right away."

3

CORAL MELLORS CLUTCHED HER SON ALL THE TIGHTER to her chest, and jumped back from the window as if shot.

"Whatever is the cause of that dreadful noise outside!?" shouted Verna, trying to scramble out of her chair, and almost spilling her precious whiskey.

"It's your son," said Coral. "And he's in a hurry." Her eyes darted around as if looking for some way to escape, but she knew that there was no escaping the problem that was Sam Mellors. In seconds he would burst through the back door, and as difficult as life had been with him gone, it was surely about to get worse.

"The worthless fruit of my loins," screamed the old woman. "As bad as his father! I'll fill his bee-hind with buckshot if he takes a hand to either one of us, mark my words, Coral, I'll *do it* this time. The days of bad trouble from the Mellors men have come to an end, I vow it to you *and* the Lord." And with that, Verna Mellors managed to lift herself out of the chair, then

staggered sideways and crashed across the room, hitting her head against the sideboard as she fell in a tangled heap on the floor.

"Horsie, Gramma, horsie," said Willie with excitement.

As Coral began to rush across the room to help the stricken woman, her husband kicked open the back door, and yelled, *"Money! Right now, and don't make me take my hand to you both."*

Verna was bleeding a steady flow of red from a cut to her temple, but the moaning coming from her was a good sign — at least she was alive. Coral needed to attend to her, but her instinct would not allow her to let Willie out of her arms.

"Horsie!"

Sam Mellors stopped in his tracks and looked at his son. He had been a baby, still crawling, when last he saw him. But the boy was of no use to him now — what he needed this instant was money. He looked at his wife. She looked afraid, yet defiant. *Always defiant.* No wonder he'd always been forced to beat her — the woman never knew when to shut her trap. Then he looked down at the floor at his mother. *Drunk as always, and bleeding.* Still, she was no use to him unconscious. *Let her bleed.*

"Please leave, Sam," said Coral. "There's nothing here for you. You know you're a *Wanted Man* in Kansas. Please! The Sheriff's not two blocks away."

He looked across at his wife as she spoke. She was a fine-looking woman. *If only I had the time,* he thought. But, lucky for Coral, he knew he had none. Coming here had been a last resort, a last desperate chance to save his skin. "Where's the money, Coral?" he asked. "There are men on my tail. I need a thousand dollars, and I know she has it hidden here somewhere. Do I have to beat it out of you?"

"Wakey wakey, Gramma," said Willie. "Gramma!"

And like magic, the old woman stirred. She blinked a few times and managed to sit up halfway, still leaned against the sideboard. She shook her head to one side then the other, as if to clear it, then looked up at her useless outlaw son and said, "Leave this house, Samuel. Or I promise you, I'll fill you so full of bullets you'll need a larger horse to carry the weight."

"Nice to see you too, Ma. But don't give me that, we all know how much you hate guns. I'm a better chance o' gettin' shot by a preacher in church than by you." He took a moment then to laugh at his own little joke, before remembering he was in a hurry. "Well, Ma, I'd love to stick around and shoot the breeze and all, but there's a posse on my trail. If I don't have a thousand dollars in my hand within one minute so's I can *buy* my way outta trouble, I'm afraid I'm gonna *have* to do somethin' nasty. And keep doin' somethin's nasty till I get that money. Now where is it?"

"Oh, son. Unobservant as well as useless," said the old woman, rubbing her fingers over her forehead then staring at the blood that dripped from them onto the floor. "I wouldn't give you that money even if there *was* any left. But if you were so much as half as observant as your father, you'd have noticed right away that most of the furniture's gone, and all the paintings as well. I sold this house nine months ago, and I've been paying the rent by selling off furniture."

She watched the look of realization dawn on her son's face as he looked around the room.

"Yes, you see it now, don't you? I had to start selling it all off to feed your wife and son, to pay rent on the house, and to keep me in whiskey, of course. No Mellors woman *ever* manages to get by without a little help from a whiskey bottle, after the way you men treat us. Except, somehow, until now, for Coral. But that can't last."

Coral had always held out, no matter how tempting whiskey seemed, when she needed to get past her troubles. She had Willie to consider. But in that moment, she saw her own future, and that of her darling son, too — if indeed Sam did not fly into a rage and cut that future short here and now. She did not like the look of the future she saw, did not like it one little bit, and Coral began then to pray, or rather, to try to make a deal with the Lord — *Get me out of this, please, Lord, and I promise you, I will do whatever...*

But that was as far as she got, before her brutal husband leaped across the room and snatched her dear son from her arms.

4

After making peace with his brothers, Roy Black rode on over from Deer Creek to visit ol' Wally Davis, and maybe talk things out a little. It was surely the right thing to do, for Wally — and his good wife Kate too — had a way of making sense of any troubling situation.

It was around noon when Roy trotted his horse down Wally's drive. It was a fine Spring day, pleasantly warm, the wildflowers in full bloom. Of course, it wasn't flowers that captivated Roy's interest — Roy was more the sort for horses, like ol' Wally himself, mostly. Maybe that was why the two of them got along so well, there always being something interesting for the pair to talk about.

Wally was sitting in the middle of his front meadow on a three-legged stool, and had heard Roy's horse coming before he saw it. The old man could identify any horse from around the town just by the clip-clopping of its hooves, a trick that had once been put to the test in the town by the use of a blindfold, and resulting in Wally ending up with quite a few dollars of a skeptic's money.

"Howdy, young Roy," called Wally as he looked up at the lone rider. He saw right away, by how the younger man was sitting his horse, that Roy wasn't as cheerful as he might be. "Beautiful day we's havin', ain't it?"

"Howdy, Wally," Roy said, dismounting his horse. "What are you doin' just sittin' in the middle of the field like that? Don't make no sense, none at all."

"Well, that's where you're wrong, young fella. I'm learnin' about bees, just takin' stock o' their habits. Might build me up a hive one o' these days, I'm thinkin'."

"What for, Wally?" said Roy, clearly surprised. "You got more money than a shovel-seller in a mining town. What's the point o' learnin' all about bees just to sell a few drops o' honey?"

"You're a good boy, but you still got a heap to learn, young Roy," Wally said with a laugh. "Money ain't what matters, not really. What matters is livin' a good life. And bees? Well, just look how happy *they* are, goin' about their daily work. Doin' just what they's meant to be doin', that's what they are. And honey's just about the best thing we can eat. It ain't about money, it's about health and happiness, and it all adds up to right livin'. Always remember that, Roy. Health and happiness — *that's* what a man wants to aim for."

Roy knelt down beside Wally's stool and studied the bees a bit too before speaking. "Well, that's kinda why I'm here, Wally. It just seems like life's passin' me by, and everyone else is finding wives and startin' up families, and gettin' their lives sorted — but me, I just keep missin' out. Why, I ain't even felt like makin' any saddles or harness lately. I'm just all outta puff, somehow. Maybe I'll leave town, try my luck elsewhere, I don't know. Just seems like this ain't the place for me, maybe."

Thing was, old Wally Davis was one step ahead of the boy. He had known Roy was troubled, had been seeing this coming for awhile, had even discussed it with his wife Kate that very morning over breakfast, and they had come to a decision. Roy Black needed direction in his life — and Wally and Kate were just the two people to provide it.

"Let's step inside and have ourselves a cup of coffee, Roy," said Wally as he got to his feet. "I hope you're hungry — *'course you are!* I could eat the antlers off a deer after all this hard work watchin' bees the past hour. Maybe Kate'll have somethin' tasty cookin' inside. Let's water this fine horse o' yours then go see."

As they watered the horse, Roy began to explain more to Wally about how he felt life was passing him by. How the other young men around the town were finding good wives, working out what they wanted to

17

do with their lives, building up their ranches and farms and so forth — and how he felt that he was not really needed by anyone, and that the world would be just as well off without him.

It was worse than even Wally had realized. Wally Davis had heard men talk like this before, and he knew it to be the sort of talk that was sometimes followed by dangerous actions, Even if Roy had been a stranger, Wally would have felt compelled to help him in some way — but truth was, Roy Black had become like a son to Wally, and a very much loved son besides. And Wally Davis was not going to sit around and let Roy wander down any wrong path if he could do something about it.

5

C ORAL M ELLORS CRIED OUT AS HER HUSBAND SNATCHED
Willie from her arms, and got a punch to the side of her
head for her trouble. *"Let him go!"* she cried, cowering
on the floor, while Sam made as if he was about to kick
her face in.

"Get out," screamed Verna. She seemed still too drunk
to stand on her feet, but by sheer force of will had
managed to get up, leaning against the sideboard for
support. The blood still flowed free from her wound,
and now she lashed out at her son with a foot. He
was wise to her tricks though, and moved too fast
for the flying boot to connect. Poor Verna lost her
balance with the effort, her body crashing to the floor
once again.

"Sure thing, I'll just be on my way," the evil man said,
holding tightly onto his squirming son as he looked
down at both women. "Soon as I get that thousand.
You're holdin' out on me, Ma, I can tell. Now where
is it? Wouldn't want the boy here to start losin' fingers,

now would we? I bet you still keep that sharp knife hidden under your bed, Ma."

Willie was a brave little boy, but he did not like the way this man had snatched him up then hit his mommy, and now he was starting to wail.

"Please, Verna," said Coral, the urgency plain in her voice. *"Please."*

"Alright," the old woman said. "Alright." The desperate situation seemed to have sobered her up some, and her voice's former nastiness was gone, replaced by something more caring, almost like love. "Oh, Sam. Son, I'm too old for all this. You'd cut your own son's fingers off, all for a few measly dollars?

"Ain't my fault, Ma. It's *you* that's to blame if it's anyone. You're *makin'* me do it, instead o' just givin' me what I need."

"Alright, son. Alright. It's not your fault, as you say. But for a different reason. It's because—"

"Shut your mouth, you old time-waster, and hurry up now — or I'll go get the knife!"

"I told you, didn't I, Coral?" said Verna. There was something strangely different about her, and Coral had never seen her look quite this way. "They're plain no good, the Mellors men, all of them. Mark my words, girl, our dear young Willie here will break your heart too some day, just as Sam and his father broke mine."

"No more talk!" Sam cried, the menace clear in his voice.

"Hold your horses, son. I've three thousand left. It's the last of your father's ill-gotten gains. I'd set it aside for young Willie's education." She sounded so old and tired. "Never knew of the safe he put in, did you? Now, before I get it, you'll agree to leave us five hundred, and never return?"

"Sure, Ma," he said. But there wasn't a one of them believed it. He would take the lot, and leave them to starve, of that they all had no doubt.

"Alright then, son. I always loved you, I want you to know it. But you're a Mellors, through and through. So it's hardly your fault you went wrong — it was in your blood from the day you were born. I just want you to know all that, before you leave — and always remember, son, always remember I love you."

"Sure, Ma," Sam said. "Now where's this safe?"

"You hand the boy back to Coral now, and help me to my feet. Then I'll open up the safe and give you the money. But then you'll leave, okay?"

"Sure, Ma. And I'll never come back, just as you say, no more trouble." He put the wailing boy down on the floor, and Willie scurried across into Coral's waiting arms.

"Wait here with Willie in the parlor, Coral. Sam, you'll help me to my room and I'll unlock the safe and give you the money. Then you'll go out by the back door."

"Just show me the safe, Ma, I'll unlock it." He was almost salivating at the thought of all that cash.

"No, Sam. I'll not give you the combination. We need you to leave us five hundred, it's going right back in the safe, and I'll not give up the combination to anyone. You'll stand back at the doorway where you can't see the numbers."

"Fine then, let's get it over with."

"Help me up, Sammy, there's a good boy."

Verna Mellors had not called her son a good boy in a very long time, and while part of what dripped down her face now was blood, it was lighter in color, more streaky than before, and some of it might have been tears.

Coral hugged her own boy tight to her chest, as she watched Sam help his Ma to her feet. The bleeding woman steadied herself against the sideboard, then walked unassisted, steadily even, out of Coral's sight as she went to her room, followed closely by Sam.

Coral's feeling of dread had never left, from the moment she went to the window, right up till now, as she sat on the floor holding her son, looking up at her husband's back as he stood in the doorway to his mother's room. It would all be over, she hoped, in less than a minute. And this time, maybe, hopefully — he would never come back.

6

Wally listened carefully to everything Roy had to say, only nodding his head and giving him such other encouragements as would keep the younger man talking. Even after they had watered the horse, Wally had Roy come for a walk across to inspect a side fence — there was nothing wrong with it, of course, it was just an excuse for them to stay outside a bit longer before going in to see Kate, as the old man wanted to hear everything Roy had to say without interruption.

At the end of it all, as they mosied along back toward Wally and Kate's home, Roy said, "My brothers don't need me no more, Wally. After our Pa died, you helped us a lot, got us through it. The boys needed me then, I reckon, to help 'em begin to make their own way in the world. But with Pa gone, and all of us out from under his heel, them three's fine now. Archie runs the farm right proper, and Marty and Milt love growin' crops near as much as he does — but you know me, I never did care much for that sorta work."

"You're a horse man like me," said Wally with a nod. "Need to be in the saddle every day, and runnin' your hands over good animals, attendin' to their every need, and doin' all you can to keep 'em in fine fettle."

Roy smiled, then cast his eye over Wally's place, and more particularly the wide range of animals that roamed around it, each getting along just fine with the others. "Yep, Wally. I'm a horse man, like you. Exceptin' that you're more an *everything* man, with horses bein' maybe even more important to you than the goats and donkeys and ducks and geese and chickens and cats and sheep and dogs and just about everything else. It's a wonder you ain't got a tiger and an elephant 'round here somewhere!"

"Wouldn't mind one each o' those to make friends with," said Wally, his eyes lighting up at the prospect. "Come on, let's head inside and see if the missus has rustled up any grub for our lunch."

"If you're finished with staring at bees all the long day," said Kate as they came through the door, "you can sit yourself down now and eat a *sensible* meal. *Honey indeed.* What sort of culinary calamities might that lead to! Plain, simple food is the best. *Honey indeed.* Hello, Roy, it's lovely to see you. Well, sit down, the pair of you, I hope you're both hungry."

As luck would have it, Kate had been baking that morning, and while her experimental potato and pumpkin and bacon pie was a little burnt at the edge, and the taste was not quite up to what Mary Bean might have cooked, there was some mighty appreciative chewing and grunting and swallowing for the next few minutes, before Wally got up from the table to clear away the plates and begin to wash them clean, while Kate poured coffee for the three of them,

"Now, down to business," said Wally, once he finished wiping the plates dry and sat back down at the table. "You was dead right, Kate, when we talked about Roy this morning."

"No need to butter me up, Wallace Erasmus Davis," she answered. "It was you who first noticed Roy wasn't so happy, but I saw it too once you said it. So, did you tell him?"

"Tell me?" asked Roy. He felt a little strange now, knowing they'd been discussing his problems — but he trusted them better than he'd ever trusted anyone else, except for maybe his Ma.

Wally gave his wife a stern look and said, "Give me a chance, Kate, I been busy—"

"Oh yes, I forgot — busy staring at bees all the day, while other people are—"

"No need to get uppity, old woman, I was only—"

"Who are you calling *old,* you ancient archaic antique atrocity? Why, I'm almost closer in age to Roy here than I am to you. If I was just a little younger, I'd have married him instead, you decrepit debilitated dawdler!"

Roy used to feel embarrassed when the Davises went at it in this manner, but he had since learned it was a game between them, and was one of the things they loved about each other. And there was no doubting the way their eyes shone whenever they were together. In fact, the fun of their little arguments was one of the reasons Roy so badly wanted a wife of his own.

That sort of happiness had eluded Roy Black his whole life so far. He had his brothers of course, and there was a tight bond between them. But before he'd met the Davises, the only real love in his life had been from his dear Ma, and she had passed on some time back, leaving Roy and his brothers at the mercy of their cruel father. His Pa had always been mean to his Ma, too, and up until Roy had gotten to know Wally, he had never thought marriage could bring such happiness.

"I'm thinkin' I'll head south. Or east maybe, or west," Roy told them. "Might find somethin' worth doin', and maybe change my luck. I'd miss you, of course, and my brothers, and my friends, and some o' the horses. But I gotta change *somethin'*, you know?"

And that's when Kate said, "Yes, Roy dear, we know. That's why we've decided — we're putting up the money for you to open a livery and saddlery in the town."

7

CORAL COULD HEAR HER MOTHER-IN-LAW TELLING Sam to stay back at the door. Willie had ceased his crying now, and she hugged him to her and watched the boy's father as he stood in the doorway — and hoped he would quietly take the money and leave.

"Stand back by the door while I pull up the boards," Verna was saying.

Coral listened to the sound of floorboards being pulled up from the floor, and watched Sam strain his neck to see.

"Let me do it, Ma," he said.

But Verna told him, "Wait there by the door till I'm done," and he did what she said. "Now, what was the combination? Oh yes, I remember. You'd laugh if you knew, son."

"Come on, Ma, there's a posse on its way, I don't have time for this.

"Yes, Sam, I know. But always remember, I love you. Never forget."

Then things went quiet for a few seconds as Verna opened up the safe, then Sam was moving out of Coral's sight, into the room toward his Ma, and Coral screamed as Sam yelled, the sound of a six-shooter rang out from the bedroom, and WIllie began to cry as Sam yelled again, "You shot me, Ma. You done shot me."

And Verna said, "It was for your own good, Sam, for your wife and your son, for us all, I'm sorry, but remember, I love you. Please! Leave now while you can, Sam."

Then came the sounds of a scuffle, and two more shots rang out, then Verna's voice, quiet yet strong, called, *"Coral. Come, dear."* And then came the sound of her coughing, a wet sound it was, and Coral knew that it couldn't be good.

She held Willie's head against her so he could not see, and she went to the room, and she saw right away Sam was dead. He must have rushed his mother as soon as she opened the safe, but she had taken the loaded gun from inside it, turned it on him as he got there, and fired it.

"Oh, Verna, what happened?"

"It all happened so fast, but I knew he'd do it. It's better this way. I thought maybe … maybe … just the shot in his arm would get him to leave. But he rushed me again — he'd never have stopped, Coral. He'd have killed you and Willie. I hope you can forgive me."

"Of course, Verna. It was self defense, we both know it."

Verna looked up into Coral's eyes, her vision beginning to fade, but she kept her resolve and went on. "Tell the Sheriff what happened here, Coral. Take the money from the safe . . . leave this terrible place forever. Start a new life, away from Kansas, away from this family, away from everything you've ever known."

She coughed a small cough, and blood sprayed from her mouth when she did so. She was dying alright.

"You'll be okay," said Coral, but she knew it was a lie. "I'll go fetch the doctor."

"I'm done for, dear. Please, stay with me," Verna said. "Is he gone, Coral? Is my boy gone now, somewhere better?"

"He is."

"Tell the Sheriff, then pay the undertaker to bury me with my son. Then leave this place, leave it and never come back. Find a man who's as different to a Mellors as you can. A banker. A clerk. A man who sells fabrics or furnishings or writes pretty words for a newspaper. Keep your boy away from horses, and wild men, and liquor, and guns — but most especially horses. Those things turn all the Mellors men to thieving, it's like gold bars lying on the ground in front of their eyes. Keep your boy away from wild men and horses, and maybe he won't turn out so much like a Mellors at all. Truth is, I don't like his chances. It's all in the blood, I reckon. Goodbye, Coral. Goodbye, little Willie, you be a good boy now for your Ma."

"No," cried Coral. *"Verna, don't leave us!"* And all too late, Coral knew just how much the woman had cared, how much she had suffered, how much she'd been torn between love for her family and the overwhelming belief that they were all bad.

Coral held the dying woman's hand, and they looked into each other's eyes — and to Coral's great surprise, she saw love, even happiness, there in the old woman's eyes — then they flickered, and Verna was gone.

8

Roy Black looked at Kate, then at Wally, then he looked away out the window, ran a hand through his hair and wiped a small tear from his eye, real quick before they could see it.

"I ... I don't know what to say." The other eye had begun to fill up too, and Roy gave it the same treatment.

Wally looked out the window as well, not wanting the youngster to know he had seen the tears forming. "You don't need to say nothin' but yes, Roy."

Roy turned back toward them. "Well, what I will say is thanks. You're generous people, the both of you, and I appreciate all you've done — for me *and* my brothers. But I can't say yes. It's one thing for family to put up such money, but another altogether—"

"Roy," said Kate. "You *are* our family. Yes, it's Henry and Rose and their children that live here in the other house, and they're family too. But you know Wally and myself never had the opportunity to have children of our own. And you, Roy — you're special to us. Don't you see, you're the son we never could have. Please say yes. Please."

"She's right, Roy," said Wally. "And you know she'll just start up with all her big words if you make her argue for it. And none of us will get *any* peace then, am I right?"

Roy thought about it some more. It was a fine idea, and much to his liking, and he knew that Wally and Kate meant just what they said. Truth was, he felt the same way about them. "In town, you say."

"In town, Roy. Just down apiece from the Milligans' mercantile. I bought the land from Max and Mabel just last week. They always had plans to branch out, you see, but now Gilbert's going to run the bank, it'd be too much for them. Emmy-Lou's too ... well, you know Emmy-Lou. She's a lovely girl, but not so much help with runnin' a business, I'd warrant. Thing is, the town needs a livery real bad — Toby Wilkinson can't be expected to try to keep up with everyone's horses as well as run the saloon, especially since Emily started up the Tea Room there as well, and him having to help out with that."

"But I don't know nothin' about business. And the town's too small to support it, surely?"

"Too small yet, but the town's growing," said Kate. "TK Waters is a smart man, Roy. He wouldn't be investing in building a bank here if he didn't know something we don't."

"That's right," said Wally. "We figure TK knows somethin', and that somethin' can only be to do with either the railroads or the stagecoach route. Makes no sense to run the railroad this way, so it must be the stage. There's all manner o' towns gettin' started to the north o' here, springin' up beside the Yellowstone. Been gold strikes more and more places too. Nothin' big yet, but it's out there, and TK knows it. This place is soon goin' to be on the map, Roy, we're quite sure of it."

"You've thought it all through then," said Roy.

"Sure have. We figure the best thing is to jump in up front with a combined livery and saddlery, and it'll be the natural choice for the stagecoach depot. TK Waters ain't the only one with a good head for business."

"But why me, Wally?"

The old man shook his head, smiled, and looked Roy right in the eye. "I'm surprised you need even to ask. But as you have, I'll tell it straight. You're good with horses, and the best young leatherworker I ever saw. Your fancy work'll sell for a premium once more people lay eyes on it, and Come-By-Chance is goin' to grow, Roy, it's goin' to grow fast, you'll soon see it. But most of all, the reason we want *you* is because you're *completely* honest — and that's a rare quality in a man."

"My family has a bad reputation 'round these parts, Wally. I'm a Black. People won't trust me, you know that."

"No, dear," said Kate. "That reputation belongs all to your father, *may he rest in peace,* whether he deserves it or not. There's not a man within fifty miles with a bad word to say about *you* — or any one of your brothers, for that matter."

"It's true, son," said Wally. "We expect to share in the profits, o' course. It's purely a business arrangement." He winked at Kate while Roy wasn't looking, and she smiled back knowingly.

"And I'll do the books, of course," said Kate. "Please say yes, Roy — I ran the Postal Office in Pittsburgh for sixteen years, you know. I miss all the paperwork, the organizing, the banking of the money. And it'll get me out of the house, away from this grizzled geriatric old goat too. You'd be doing us both a great favor. Yes, Wally's wonderful in small doses, but getting me away from the desultory dunderhead a few times a week might even give us time to miss each other, and strengthen up an otherwise flimsy marriage."

"It's true," said Wally. "Why, our whole marriage is based only on my good looks. It's a well known fact."

"Yes," said Kate. "I always did want a monkey for a pet." And this time it was Kate's turn to wink.

Roy looked at them both and held back the tears.

He knew they were making some of it up, of course. He figured, too, that his family's reputation would be tied to that of his father for a good many years to come — and that he would have to work hard and be the most honest man ever there was to retrieve it.

But he realized, too, that the feeling of excitement and joy inside him might be a great force for good. And also that — while he had only recently become one for church — the Lord had surely set things up this way, and only a fool would not go along with it.

So Roy Black looked first to Wally, and then to Kate, and he said, "Thank you, both of you. It's a deal. I promise, I won't let you down." And it was a good thing that Kate rushed over then to hug him, for the tears he'd held back had started to run, and it didn't seem right to Roy for Wally to see them.

9

Coral Mellors had been through a terrible time, to be sure.

She had known for a long while now that her decision to marry Sam had been a bad one — but in the beginning, he had been charming and intelligent, clean and well-dressed, and had such a way with words that she had fallen for him right away.

It had not taken long for her to find out the truth about him — that he was a rogue, a gambler, a mean drunk, and a horse-thief into the bargain. But by then it was too late. By then she was in the family way, cut off from what family and friends she had known back East, and all she could do was try to stay out of his way whenever he was drunk.

Verna had done her best to protect Coral and Willie — she saw that now. Coral had never thought she cared, had thought the woman only allowed them to stay with her from a sense of duty. But in the end, Verna had given her own life, and taken that of her own no-good son, just so Coral and Willie could be safe.

It was the ultimate sacrifice — and one that Coral knew she could never have made herself, no matter what. She owed it to Verna to listen to the woman's last words, to at least *try* to do what she'd said.

So that was just what Coral did. The Mellors home wasn't far from the Courthouse, and the Sheriff came right away, having heard the shots Verna had fired. He was an astute man, and saw in an instant what had happened — Verna Mellors' no-good horse-thieving son had come back and demanded money, and the woman had gone to her safe then turned her gun on him when he attacked her.

The Sheriff did not allow Coral to speak first, as he normally would have when investigating a crime. Instead, after looking at the bodies in the bedroom, he came out to the parlor and told Coral his *own* version of what had happened as clearly as he could manage. He nodded his head slowly as he said it, to suggest that she should simply go along with the words he was saying.

"No sense laying blame on anyone here," he told her. "Verna had it hard enough in life, without having anyone think her a murderer now she's gone. Agreed, Coral?"

"Yes, Sheriff Tomson. Thank you." She was shaking, now it was over, and it was all sinking in. And Willie, for his part, was clinging to her like a new baby possum to its momma.

"Coral, I...I don't want this to come out wrong, and I have your best interests at heart — yours as well as the boy's."

"Yes, Sheriff?"

"It's just...well, the name Mellors has been mud in this town for a long while, and that sorta mud sticks a long, long time. Generations. I'd hate to see your young tadpole never get a fair chance in life on account of his father and grandfather's evildoings. I'll do my best to help if you stay, but I just wonder if you might be best served moving on. Do you have family you could go to?"

"I have a cousin in Boston, but — Sheriff, the truth is, my whole family disowned me when I married Sam. I doubt they'd take me in if I went back there anyway."

"That's what I figured. No offense to Verna, but it makes sense you'd have already left if you had someplace worth going. Same thing happened to Verna — disowned by her family for marrying a Mellors, did you know?"

Coral looked across at the sideboard, Verna's blood still on it. "She never told me that, Sheriff."

"She was a good woman, you know, before she made that one bad choice. Still ended up with this house when her father passed, though. There was no one else for him to leave it to. You know she sold it to a banker a few months back?"

"Yes, Sheriff, I know."

"Anyway, here's a suggestion, take it or leave it," the Sheriff said, scratching his head as he did so. "I know a woman in Omaha — fine woman, name of Beryl Waters. Smart as a whip. First met her in Pittsburgh, when we were a whole lot younger. She was a banker then, believe it or not. Anyway, I thought she was the best catch this side of the Mississippi. Well, she woulda been. Turned out, she wasn't the marrying kind, and it was my great loss, I'll tell you. But now, Beryl lives up in Omaha. Runs some sort of art and music society there. But more importantly, she takes in women from time to time, women with children too, if they're in need — and she helps them get back on their feet. Fine woman. The finest there is."

"You think she'd help us?"

"I won't mention names, it being imprudent, but I've twice sent women to her before, and I can promise you, they're both doing fine. More importantly, Beryl made me promise to do so again, if I know of any woman who needs it. Truth is, young Coral, I was just about to intervene and see if you'd go to her, right before Sam got run out of town two years back. But once he was gone, I figured you and Verna could look after each other, and I stayed out of it. Will you go, Coral? I think it could make all the difference, especially for that little tadpole in your arms. He deserves a chance in life, and so do you, girl, so do you. Don't let Verna's passing be in vain. She was a fine woman before she got mixed up with Frank Mellors, I promise you that."

For one short moment then, a slice of a sliver of a fraction of a fragment of a thought jumped into Coral's head, something to do with the unfinished prayer she had almost managed earlier, and with it came a feeling of rightness — there had been so little rightness for Coral and Willie since he'd come along — so she looked at kind Sheriff Tomson, said, "Yes please," and burst into tears. And for the whole next hour, she cried all the tears that had been building up inside her for the four longest years of her life.

10

It was with mixed feelings that Coral Mellors stood out in the drizzling rain, attending the burial of her husband and his mother.

It was a small turnout, just Coral and the Sheriff and a few old-timers Verna had known for years — people who knew the real Verna, before the hard realities of becoming a Mellors had taken its toll.

Coral didn't much listen as the preacher spoke, her thoughts drifting this way and that, as she tried to make sense of it all.

When she had first met Sam, she had thought him the most charming and wonderful man she'd ever met. Her feelings for him had rushed all over the top of her, and all the wise counsel in the world was just so much noise in the background, as far as Coral was concerned.

She had simply not wanted to hear it.

At the time, she figured her friends and family to be jealous that she would be lucky enough to have met such a man. In fact, the strong feeling she'd had then, that nobody else understood, the feeling that it was she and Sam against the whole world, had only served to make their situation seem all the more romantic — and she had run away with him, even after being told she would be disowned if she ever saw him again.

That was almost four years ago. She had married him the very next day, but it was a week before she found out he had stolen the good silverware from her home while they were in the very act of eloping. It was two weeks before they had *really* had to go on the run, that being to do with a stolen horse — Sam assured her it was a case of mistaken identity, and that the accusers were just out to get him, on account of him having bested them in a fair business deal. But when the same thing happened in two other states, Coral began to realize that the charming Sam Mellors was not exactly the friendly, honest fellow she'd thought he was.

He lied and robbed his way from one side of the country halfway across to the other, leaving a whole trail of disgruntled people behind him, and by the time they'd arrived in Kansas, Coral had just about had enough. She was already in the family way, and more than once she had tried to leave.

But every time she brought it up, Sam would promise to change his ways, and tell her stories of how good their life would be once they went home to Kansas.

He'd tell her of the fine house he lived in, and all about how his father was a highly respected businessman, and his mother was from the richest family in Kansas, and that when they went "home" he would get a good job and "go straighter than an Indian's arrow."

Well, the part about the fine house had been true.

Also, Verna had been from a well-to-do family, which is how they'd managed to come by the fine house in the first place.

But Sam's father, if anything, was even more of a no-gooder than Sam, and just as charming when out and about — but at home the man was a terror, brutally beating Verna on a regular basis.

It was just the way things were, and there was nowhere to escape to anyway.

For Sam's part, he found himself a job as promised — stealing horses with his father. Then one night, Sam had come home alone, his father having made a fatal mistake, and receiving a well-earned bullet through his brain.

Verna had cried at the funeral, stood there and cried like the most loving wife ever there was, and at the time, Coral had thought it most strange.

Yet here, now, Coral stood in that same place, and she too was crying as they lowered her own husband into *his* grave.

And now, finally, Coral Mellors understood.

It had *not* been her brutal no-good husband that Verna had cried for, Coral saw that quite clearly now —she had cried for her son, had cried for the knowledge that one day, it would be him, for she knew that he too would die a bad death for his sins, and that nothing she could ever do would change it.

And now, sheltering under the Sheriff's umbrella, Coral watched as, first Sam, then Verna herself, were lowered into their graves. She prayed to dear God that he might hear her, and intervene in some way, make it so that her own son, her dear, sweet young Willie, would somehow be different — and she vowed to do whatever she could to help.

And as she threw the first, symbolic handful of dirt into Verna's grave, she whispered, "Thank you, dear Verna. I promise, your death won't be in vain."

11

Within three days, Coral and Willie Mellors were alighting from the train in Omaha with everything they owned. It was late afternoon, and it seemed like everyone who had ever known the railway existed had turned up here right now for some reason.

Sheriff Tomson had wired ahead, and Beryl Waters knew the situation, and was waiting on the busy train platform to meet them.

Even if she had not had the Sheriff's description of Coral to go by, even if she had not been carrying a sleeping child, Beryl would have known which one she was right away.

The girl had the beaten, worn-down look about her that even the most courageous of abused women get, and Beryl had come to know it at a glance. She never could understand what it was that made some men treat women that way, never could work out what it was they got from it. All she knew was, it took a long time for women to get over it, if they ever did at all, really.

At least this one had a child to care for. If there was one thing Beryl did know, it was that people get over things better if they have someone *else* to look out for.

"You must be Coral," she said to the young woman.

"Yes, I... thank you, Miss Waters. We'll try not to be a burden and—"

"Now, that's no way to get started," Beryl scolded gently. "First thing, always call me Beryl—" And she leaned in conspiratorially toward Coral and, with a twinkle in her eye said, "—I get too many marriage proposals when people start calling me Miss."

Something about the way she had said it put the nervous young woman at ease right away, and Beryl was most relieved to see the girl's shoulders relax, and even allow herself a little laughter.

"Okay, Beryl, I certainly will. Thank you. And this is Willie. I'm surprised he's not woken, he's usually so inquisitive."

"Must be worn out from the travel," said Beryl. "Well, let's get your luggage and get on home. You and Willie will have your own room in the main house, and are welcome to stay as long as you need to. But, that said, what we really want to do is work together to find you a good situation — no sense wasting your life staying with an old spinster. But rest assured, dear, there's no hurry. I'm sure we'll get along just fine, and you'll have no trouble making new friends here — when you're ready, of course."

To Coral, the whole situation felt somehow strange and unnatural. But not just because she was in a strange place — everything about the world seemed somehow different, like a weight had been lifted from her shoulders, almost like some magical spell had been cast over them all.

Then she decided she was just tired from the travel herself, and that everything would seem real enough again once Willie woke up and wanted his lunch or wanted to play, and it surely would not be too long.

One thing *was* strange though — even though there were hundreds of people about, everyone seemed to know Beryl. The ladies would smile, the men would tip their hats and say, "Afternoon, Beryl," and in no time flat, two strong young men had offered to help with Coral's luggage, carrying it all to Beryl's fine coach before being rewarded with a coin each for their trouble.

It was not until they had arrived at Beryl's beautiful home that Willie woke up.

He blinked his sleepy eyes, looked at Beryl Waters, and said, "Gramma."

"Oh dear," Coral said. "No, Willie, it's not Gramma."

"It's okay," Beryl told her. "Hello, Willie. What a good boy you are. I'm sure we'll be great friends, you and me. Can you guess what my name is?"

"Gramma," said the boy, rubbing his eyes once again.

"How about you call me Aunt Beryl, yes? I bet you're hungry! We have lots of good things to eat. Are you hungry?"

"Gramma," he said, and this time he smiled a smile that melted Beryl Waters' heart in a way that no grown man's smile ever could.

"I'm so sorry," said Coral. "He's not usually this way."

"He's wonderful," Beryl told her. "Don't you worry what he calls me. I know what happened to you in Kansas, and we don't have to talk about it at all, Coral dear, unless you decide that you want to. But it seems to me, if he needs to call me Gramma, we might just let him, yes? But you're his mother, and in all things to do with your child, it's up to you to decide."

"Thank you," said Coral. "I guess it won't hurt for now." And she decided, however this had all come about, whether it was her prayers being answered or something else entirely, she and her son were lucky to be here with this kind woman, and everything would surely soon work out okay.

12

It was the Sabbath, the weather was good, and just about everyone from in and around Come-By-Chance was in church.

This was partly on account of Preacher Ernest James Coy being about as fine a Preacher as the Lord ever put breath into — and partly on account of there being an important town meeting scheduled for immediately after the service.

The newly built church was a good bit fancier than the old one. TK Waters had put up more than enough money to rebuild it after the fire that had almost claimed the lives of most of the townsfolk just a few months ago. It was a better design too — even though the notorious outlaw Slim Jim Murdoch was safely locked away doing twenty years hard labor, it would have been plain stupid to make the same mistakes as last time. And so, the new church had been built with three exits instead of one, and with no possible way of barring the doors from the outside.

No sense taking chances, everyone figured, especially as a bank would soon be built in the town — for wherever you put a bank, you tend to attract the sort of people who think they just might be able to rob it.

The new church was bigger too. Again, with the town going ahead, and about to have a bank of its own, all sorts of other business was likely to follow — and that's what this Town Meeting was all about

It was time to elect the first ever Mayor of Come-By-Chance.

Preacher Coy, being that very best sort of a Preacher, the sort who doesn't just go through the motions, but makes each service count according to current needs, was making use of the service to preach all about how Jesus cared more about the *Common Good* than he did about lining his own pockets.

Soon after he had gotten started, the Preacher had noticed a steady stream of strangers beginning to file in, and indeed, it was the biggest turnout a Come-By-Chance church service had ever seen, even bigger than when TK Waters had imported all manner of performers for his daughter Emmy-Lou's wedding to Gilbert Milligan a while back.

The Preacher was not the only one to notice these late arrivals. Even though it felt somewhat strange to him in this new larger church, Ben Wilkinson had retained his old habit of always seating himself in the very back row, it seeming like the best place to keep an eye on things, just in case anyone decided to get up to no good.

And so, Ben and his wife Lettie had watched, first with interest, then with amazement, as stranger after stranger walked into the church and took their seats toward the back — but on the right hand side — until there were almost a dozen of them.

They had come in quietly enough, and while they were dusty from their ride, each man had removed his hat in the correct and respectful manner. There had been extra strangers in town lately, for small amounts of gold had been found here and there, the biggest strike being about thirty miles east — but even so, strangers tended to come in dribs and drabs, not a whole lot at once like this.

It was probably nothing, but still, it looked like trouble to Ben. He was having a hard time bringing his attention back to the Preacher since the men had started traipsing into the church, for even though they *seemed* respectable enough, all but one of them looked wiry and strong, and the only one who didn't had a certain air about him, a certain something that left no doubt he was the man in charge.

On the day of the town's first ever elections to decide on a Mayor, this development, Ben decided, could only mean trouble. He had heard stories of such things happening in small towns before, and it surely looked like a power play of some sort to Ben's mind. And so, instead of listening to Preacher Coy's fine words, Ben focussed instead on figuring what might be done if these new arrivals were here to tip the voting for Mayor one way or another.

13

THE FIRST DAY OR TWO, FEELING SAFER THAN SHE HAD felt in a very long time, Coral slept longer and more soundly than she had in years.

For the first two days she stayed in the house, never venturing outside to walk through the gardens or look at the surroundings.

Besides, there was so much to see inside. Beryl was an artist, a photographer, a musician, and the house was filled with all manner of wonderful art. Some of the art had been done by Beryl and her live-in housekeeper, Hattie; some was fine art by famous painters, collected by Beryl over the years; and some had been purchased by Beryl from local women who she herself had taught how to paint.

It puzzled Coral that some of the art was not very good, but what she did not know was that buying this art was Beryl's way of helping some people without it seeming like charity.

Still, however Coral felt about the art, she herself

felt safer than she had in years, having satisfied herself that Beryl and Hattie, as well as the other two young women currently staying in the mansion, were all good people. Best of all, she did not have to worry about *men* intruding in her own life, and more importantly, Willie's.

Yes, with her husband in his grave, and having been assured that Beryl enforced a strict No Men Allowed rule for the main house, it seemed to Coral as if she could finally relax, safe in the knowledge that no harm would come to herself or her child.

And she *slept.*

Willie, though, was the opposite. He had done more than his fair share of sleeping on the train. And now he seemed determined to make up for it by staying awake as long as he possibly could.

It helped, too, that he had Beryl to talk to and play with, and that she was a most willing participant in his games. The highly animated youngster still insisted on calling her Gramma, and while Beryl would never have asked for a child to do so, she could not help feeling glad about it. For a woman with no children of her own, being called Gramma was an unexpected delight — and so was Willie himself.

Beryl Waters was a self-made woman, a millionaire if anyone was counting, although she did not brag about any of that. Originally from Pittsburgh, she had been one of the smartest and shrewdest bankers to ever set up an investment, but making money had brought her no joy whatsoever. While still at a young enough age to enjoy the money she'd earned, she left the banking business in her brother's capable hands, and the famous TK Waters, while not being nearly as clever as Beryl herself, had done well enough for himself and his family.

Beryl had moved away then to Omaha, having heard that it was a lively sort of place for painters and musicians and the like — and also that people of all types, from many different countries, were moving there to make interesting lives for themselves.

The proof of that pudding had been in the eating, and she had indeed built for herself the exact sort of life she really wanted.

After the boring world of finance, the diversity of Omaha had been the perfect tonic for Beryl. And while she would never have children of her own, she had been able to help many people, both as a patron of the arts and on a personal level. And quite rightly, she was without doubt highly respected all about town.

If Coral had known, though, what Beryl and Willie were doing this very moment, she would not have been nearly as impressed by Beryl as most people were, and indeed, she would have woken from her catnap with a start.

With Coral needing to catch up on sleep, Beryl had foregone attending her usual midday church service, as someone had to look after Willie. She had considered waking Coral, but decided against it — Beryl saw nothing wrong with them missing out on church just this once, but if the girl felt compelled to attend, they could just as easily attend an evening service.

It was one of the things Beryl loved about Omaha — with all the different nationalities living in their own little pockets of the city, such as Little Italy, Greek Town, Sheelytown, Little Poland and Little Bohemia, there was always some sort or other of interesting church service to attend, at all different times of the day.

And Beryl always had been of the belief that a bit of variety spiced up an interesting life.

There was an hour yet before several local women were due to arrive for the Sunday afternoon music session Beryl always hosted after church. Willie had become restless and noisy in the way all healthy almost-three-year-old boys do. Not wishing the boy to disturb Coral's rest, Beryl took him by the hand and led him outside for a walk through the grounds.

It was an extra-large block, with well maintained gardens, all lovingly tended by old Frank Wilson, a neighbor who'd been down on his luck before Beryl had moved there. He had been about to lose his home, and Beryl had a good feeling about him. She offered him a job looking after the grounds and her horses, plus maintaining the house for her, on the condition he move into the living quarters attached to the barn. And they had both been happy with the arrangement ever since.

Beryl and Willie walked through the grounds now, the little boy delighting at the trees and the grass, the bees and the butterflies. But when they rounded the corner of the barn, and Willie spied a magnificent white mare grazing in her paddock, he became more excited than Beryl had known he could become.

"Horsie! Horsie! Horsie!"

And he broke into a run, eager as he was to get to the animal, and Beryl's old legs were barely able to catch him up before he had made it through the post and rail fence and into the horse's yard.

"Whoa, boy," Beryl said as she caught him, holding him back from the fence as best she could. "You like horses, do you?"

"Horsie, Gramma! Horsie!"

Beryl found herself so caught up in Willie's excitement, before she knew it she'd said, "Would you like a little ride on the horsie?"

"Horsie!"

Yes, clearly he would, she thought.

"Frank," she called. "Oh, Frank, are you around?"

Frank was having a short rest himself when Beryl called out, but he was only too happy to do whatever Beryl asked, and a minute later, for the very first time in his life, William Timothy Mellors found himself, to his own great excitement, sitting high on the back of a horse, feeling just like a king of the world.

14

I T WAS DOUBTFUL THAT EITHER FRANK WILSON OR Beryl Waters had ever seen a boy with a more joyous expression than that worn by young Willie Mellors as he sat astride that huge white horse. It was unlikely that such a young boy had ever felt quite so grand as Willie did in this moment.

He had no way to describe it, of course, but in later years he would relate the feeling of his first time on a horse as being *the feeling of his destiny rushing over him.*

He would remember it always: the way his fingers felt the softness of the horse's coat; the way its mane swished about; the strength and sheer aliveness he felt run from that horse to himself as it moved — and the smell, always he'd remember the smell, the most perfect and exciting smell he had ever known.

Yes, Willie's joy in that moment could not have been stronger.

Frank kept a good hold of him, keeping him safe, while Beryl walked the horse around slowly — and strangely, Willie made no sound at all, the feeling of being *right where he belonged* somehow working to quiet the usually talkative boy.

He smiled, he grinned, he beamed his delight — but not a chuckle or a chortle or even the tiniest giggle came from his lips. He was simply so caught up in the absolute bliss of the moment, no word or sound could do it justice.

They walked the mare around for a good five minutes, and when Beryl drew the horse to a full stop and said, "I think that's enough horsie for one day," he did not utter a word of complaint, but only asked, "Again?"

Beryl answered, "Tomorrow, if you're a good boy. The horsie is very tired now, and Frank has to give her some food."

But just as Frank went to lift the boy down from the horse, a terrible scream assailed all of their ears, the noise of it scaring both Willie and the old horse so badly that both jumped in different directions, the result being that Willie's behind and the white mare's back parted company, and the boy began to plummet headlong toward the ground.

It was a lucky thing indeed that Frank Wilson's reflexes were good, that he did not scare easy, and that his head stayed cool in any sort of emergency.

As Willie jumped with a start at his approaching mother's scream, the terrified horse had jumped sideways, away from the noise — but Frank had maintained just enough grip on the boy to save him, albeit at the cost of his own balance. In the end it was Frank who ended up splayed out on his back on the grass, with Willie coming to rest on top of the old man, completely unharmed.

"Mommy *scare* horsie!" said Willie. *"Naughty Mommy!"*

"What is the *meaning* of this?" cried Coral as she ran across the grounds, before scooping Willie up into her arms and saying, "Are you hurt, Willie? My poor baby boy! What did that *nasty* horse do to you?"

"Please calm yourself, Coral dear," said Beryl, rubbing the agitated old mare's muzzle to soothe her jangled nerves. She was a quiet and lovely horse, but was not accustomed to people screaming hysterically nearby, and had gotten quite a shock.

"Calm myself?" said Coral, clearly irrational. "How can I be calm, when the moment I turn my back you place my son in grave danger? You almost killed him!"

Frank was slowly getting to his feet now, grateful his old bones had managed to react quickly enough to avert the disaster Coral's screaming had caused. While he was a placid and gentle sort of man, he was protective of kind Beryl Waters, and besides, he always was one to give credit — and for balance, blame also — where it was due. "If you'll pardon my interrupting, young lady, the boy was perfectly safe, up until you yourself let loose that bloodcurdling scream and frightened both him and the horse."

"How *dare* you lay the blame on me!" said Coral. "You had *no* right to even be *near* my son, let alone put him up on the back of that dangerous beast."

"Horsie, Mommy, horsie," said Willie. He was quite clearly over the scare, and reaching his arms out toward the white mare, wanting only to be near her again.

"Coral," said Beryl, "if you wish to blame someone, I'll wear it. But I won't have you accusing Frank of anything. He's a good man, and you have no right to blame him. Besides which, he's right — the child was happy and safe, and your own screaming was the cause of the fall. Why, Frank *saved* him! If anything, you should be thanking the man. If not for Frank, yes, it might well have been a disaster."

"I came here to keep Willie *away* from men and horses, and *now* look what's happened," cried Coral. She burst into tears then, and with Willie squirming in her arms to try to keep sight of the horse, she ran off inside to her room.

15

Preacher Ernest James Coy loved nothing better than to help others, and preaching was just one of the ways he did so. And sometimes, during a service, he was happy to talk on and on if he thought it was doing some good.

But today was not one of those days.

For one thing, most of the townsfolk were already on edge when they arrived, eager to get to the special business of the day, the Town Meeting, where they would elect themselves a Mayor.

But now, for a second thing, a whole bunch of strangers had walked into the church and taken seats up the back — and while Ernest hoped for the opportunity to preach to these strangers again, his own curiosity about what had brought them to Come-By-Chance was rising up inside him, making it difficult to concentrate and give of his best.

And besides, for a third thing, the ever-observant Sheriff Johnson and his equally vigilant new wife, Opal, had also noticed the men — in spite of their best efforts at quietness — as they'd walked in. And Ernest could tell the Johnsons were eager to get to the bottom of what all these newcomers were up to.

And so it was that, after just a small amount of speaking and having everyone sing just one quick hymn, Preacher Coy wrapped up the service in double-quick time — and almost a dozen newcomers missed out on the chance to hear the finest Preacher in the Territory at his inspirational best.

"I'd like to conclude today's service," Ernest said, "by thanking you all for coming, and reminding some of you that we are, indeed, here *every* Sunday, not just when there's a wedding or a Town Meeting. But even more importantly, until we meet again, remember that the Good Lord loves you all, not just while you're in church, but every second of every day of your lives — and he'd have you all care just as much for each other. So today, when you vote for a Mayor, think of what's best for everyone, not just for yourself. There will now be a ten minute recess, then we'll all reconvene here for the Town Meeting."

One unkempt old-timer was heard then to say, "I ain't so sure I wanna come back for that, less'n someone explains jus' what this ree-cum-veenerin' thing might be. Sounds a mite painful, in fact." This comment served to lighten the moment considerably, leading to much good-natured laughter as it did so.

Some folk took the opportunity to head outside and stretch their legs, or get some fresh air, or have a smoke — the latter leading to an immediate reduction in the freshness of the air — and when they did so they saw that, not only were there a dozen new men in the town, but that they had arrived with a whole lot of wagons carrying all manner of building materials.

The visiting men had been first to step back outside, of course, but the three Wilkinson brothers, Ben Matt and Toby, along with Bert Harrison and Sheriff Calvin Johnson, were itching to get to the bottom of what they were doing in town. But before the locals could even introduce themselves to the new arrivals, Emmy-Lou Milligan, wife of Gilbert and daughter of TK Waters the banker, had rushed past them all and jumped into the arms of the eldest of the newcomers, a somewhat portly fellow who was quite obviously the head man.

Emmy-Lou squealed with delight as she landed in the man's strong grasp. *"Uncle Maurice, you're here, you're finally here!"*

16

Uncle Maurice might have been a bit past his prime and carrying more than a few extra pounds, but the strength of the man was obvious. He spun Emmy-Lou around and threw her into the air as if she were a small child, before placing her gently back on the ground and holding her out at arm's length.

"Let me look at you," he said in a deep growly voice, before tilting his head this way and that, as the excited young woman turned in a circle in front of him then bobbed a neat little curtsy. "Marriage agrees with you, I see. Now where's this husband of yours?"

"Oh yes, you simply *must* meet my darling Gilbert. *Gilbert! Wherever have you gotten to?* Oh, *there* you are," she said, as the young man pushed his way through the crowd that had gathered around Emmy-Lou and the large bear-like man.

"Whatever is going on, Emmy-Lou?" asked Gilbert. They were words he was getting used to asking. "And who *are* all these men?"

"Oh, Gilbert, you sillykins, it surely could not be more obvious. It's my Uncle Maurice and his men, of course. Oh, Uncle, it's *so* wonderful to see you. Although I doubt I shall even *speak* to you the whole time you're here, for it was *ever* so cruel of you not to come to my wedding."

"Oh, Emmy-Lou," said Maurice, "I explained all that at the time, and your father assures me he explained it to you over and over. So, Gilbert." He reached his huge hand out for Gilbert to shake, then proceeded to almost crush the young man's hand in his own as he did so. "You're a lucky man. And one with an excellent punch, TK tells me over and over. To tell you the truth, I've often felt like planting one on TK myself — even as good a friends as we are."

"Nice to meet you, sir. But I assure you, I only hit Mister Waters because I had to, and it'll never happen again."

"Well, that's a discussion for some other time, perhaps once we've sorted out business. I see we've arrived just before a Town Meeting, so of course, we'll leave the business part till right after. But I trust you have everything ready."

"Ready?" asked the bewildered Gilbert Milligan. "Business? I'm sorry, but... Emmy-Lou, who is this man, and what's going on?"

"Oh, Gilbert Milligan, I never did *meet* such a *silly* man. Why, I already told you, this is my dear Uncle Maurice."

"But Emmy-Lou," said Gilbert, "you don't *have* any uncles, just an Aunt Beryl."

"Well of *course* I do. We *all* can see him right here in front of us. Oh dear, why *ever* did I marry such a silly, silly boy? In fact, your eyes must be quite awful if you can't even see him — I mean, just *look* at the very *size* of him! *However* did you get so fat, Uncle? And *old* too. Why, your hair has gone grayer than Wally Davis's horse. Oh, Uncle, you simply *must* see all the tricks he can do!"

"Wally Davis or the horse?" asked Uncle Maurice, the smile spreading out all over his face now, for Emmy-Lou never ceased to amuse him.

"Why, the *horse* of course. Why would Wally Davis do tricks? Why, Uncle, I *do* declare, you're *almost* as silly as Gilbert!"

Most of the townsfolk were well amused by the whole conversation, for by now they were used to Emmy-Lou's strange way of speaking, and the way she would begin to speak about one thing and end up talking about another sort of thing altogether.

But Gilbert, being more responsible than most, and aware that time was running out before the Town Meeting must begin, was determined to get to the bottom of all this right away.

"Emmy-Lou Milligan," he said. "I *do* love you, but please stop talking, just for one minute, right now!"

She went to speak again, of course, but Gilbert had anticipated it, and from his pocket he produced a bag of lemon drops, and quicker than a snake-strike, he popped four of them into his wife's mouth as soon as she opened it.

"There you go, your favorite," he said, then turned to the bear-like man in front of him and said, "Emmy-Lou has no uncle, I'm sure. Who are you, and why are you here?"

"I see what's happened," said the big man with a laugh. "I'm Maurice Carlson, and you're right, I'm not her *real* uncle, but I'm her godfather, and she's family to me if anyone is. I told TK to send the letter direct to you, but he insisted his daughter would never forget to inform her husband of a thing of such importance. Me and my men are here to build the bank, and you, young Gilbert, are supposed to have everything ready for us."

"Oh yesh," said Emmy-Lou through her mouthful of lemon drops. "I musht have forgot."

"*Emmy-Lou!*" said Gilbert. "I sometimes wonder if there's anything *at all*—"

"Time for the meeting, everyone," called Preacher Ernest James Coy from the front of the church. "Please make your way back inside."

17

After giving Coral some time to think about things, Beryl went to the younger woman's room and tapped lightly on the door. "Coral, dear," she called gently. "Can we talk a moment?"

Coral walked over and opened the door. "I'm so sorry, Beryl," she said. "I didn't mean to be rude. It's just..."

"I understand, dear," Beryl told her. "I see Willie's having a catnap. He looks *so* precious when he's sleeping, doesn't he! Shall we have a nice cup of tea and talk in the parlor? The ladies will be here soon for our Sunday afternoon music session."

Hattie had already made the tea, and almost like magic, there it was, a beautiful steaming teapot and two matching china cups, in a cozy nook in the corner of the large, richly furnished room. As parlors went, the one in Beryl Waters' home was the largest in Omaha, almost half the size of a ballroom.

"Before we begin, Coral," Beryl told her as they took

their seats, "please be assured this entire conversation will stay between us. I won't repeat it, not to anyone. Hattie is in the kitchen preparing the afternoon tea, and Lillie and Pearl aren't due back from church for a good twenty minutes. Our privacy is complete."

"Thank you, Beryl."

Coral seemed awkward about what had happened, but the older woman knew it was important for them to discuss it. If they simply ignored it, she knew it would fester and ruin their chance of a proper friendship, rendering Beryl unable to help the girl and her son.

"Coral," she said as she poured the steaming, rich-smelling tea, "I'm going to just come right out with it. Willie's *your* son, and no one, not me or anyone else, has a right to tell you how to raise him. It's important that you understand, whatever happens, I will *always* do my best to help you. There's too much bad treatment of women in society, and if some of us don't step up and *do* something, that's never going to change. Me, I can't do much. I take in a few women such as yourself — I won't tell you details of *why* Pearl and Lillie are here, just as I won't tell them why *you're* here. But what I *can* do is supply a safe place to stay for awhile, and try to help each of you to find your *own* way. I can't do it *for* you, and to be truthful, the less time you're here the better off you'll be."

"I don't understand," said Coral. Her heart sank now, it seeming almost like Beryl was telling her she'd have to move on. "So you wish us to leave?"

"No, no," Beryl said, "dear oh dear, wait a moment, that came out the wrong way. You *can* stay for as long as you need to — but the sooner you learn that you don't *need* to, the better off you'll be. Thing is, dear, we all have to live in the world. Take me for instance — I was a hotshot banker when I was young, made more money than anyone could imagine. Used to get marriage proposals week in week out, some of them from *good* men. A few anyway. But I never wanted that, *any* of it. People looked at my life and thought I was happy — but it wasn't the case, not at all."

"But surely—"

"Surely nothing, Coral. You see, I hated my life. I was drowning in the life I'd built, because I wasn't doing it *for* me. It was the life I *thought* I should have, do you understand what I'm saying? The life my mother wanted for me, and not what I wanted myself. She was poor, you see? And my dear mother, she used to tell me, all the time, get ahead, Beryl. Make your own way, but bow down where you have to, marry a powerful man, make good decisions, become *rich*. Always work hard, and put yourself in a position where nothing can hurt you."

"But surely that was sound advice," said Coral. She

was so intrigued by the conversation she had completely forgotten to sip her tea.

"Part of it, perhaps," said Beryl. "The *make your own way* part. But even then, only partly. You see, I wasn't being *me*. My mother's fears were so great, she felt compelled to put them into me too — and it almost took my life away from me. Drink your tea, dear, you look a little faint."

Coral sat back in her chair then and sipped the refreshing tea a little, as she'd been told, then put down the cup and said, "So what happened?"

"Against my better judgment, I'd said *Yes* to a marriage proposal. A rival banker, in fact. Oh, what an alliance it would have been! Wonderful for business. The future of both our families was assured."

"Please go on," said Coral, creeping forward once again to the edge of her seat.

"It was the night before the wedding, and I was *sick* with worry. I could hear my mother's voice all through my head, of course — all her advice, all her fears, filling me up so full I could no longer breathe. But somehow, the *real* me refused to be silenced. From somewhere deep down inside me came a small voice, a voice so *tiny* it struggled to be heard, overrun as it was by all the others — my father's, my mother's, even that of my betrothed."

"What did the voice say?" Coral asked, breathless with anticipation.

"*No,*" said Beryl, so softly Coral almost didn't hear it. Then, louder, stronger, she said it again. "*No.* The one word, over and over and over again, until it filled my head with a madness that seemed like it might never leave. And at some point I began to say it then shout it then scream it."

"Goodness," said Coral, enthralled.

"They thought I'd gone quite mad, of course," Beryl told her. "Fetched the doctor, tried to tie me to the bed, everything. They almost locked me up, you know. Tried to. But by morning, I knew what had happened. That small voice began to get louder. I don't know if that voice was the Lord's or my own, but it was the one voice that mattered. Do you want to know why?"

"*Why?*"

"Because this is *my* life. That's why. And Coral … your life is *yours.* But, dear, I'm so sorry, but you need to hear this — Willie's *isn't.* His life is his own. I know you have fears for him, and that's completely natural. And I know his father was no good. And I know, too, you're afraid he'll turn out the same. Sheriff Tomson's a good man, and he told me how Verna used to talk. I know how things must have been for you, oh yes, I know. But Willie *isn't* his father, dear — he's *himself.*

He's a *beautiful* little boy, but you can't shut him up inside a tower like a fairy princess then expect him to survive when the going gets tough — and it *will*. It always does, no matter how well we hide. Willie needs his *own* life, and to learn his *own* way. You can keep him away from men and horses all you like, but if you do, in the end, he'll *hate* you for it, I promise. And the day he's old enough to leave you, off he'll go, running toward them, and your fears will have only made things worse, because he'll never have learned how to handle horses, or men either for that matter — and then he *will* end up trampled, by one or the other, it's true."

The two women were quiet then for several seconds, and Beryl knew that Coral was seeing the sense of it, but struggling too. She decided to tell her just one more thing.

"Coral. I left Pittsburgh a month after all that. It was a terrible time. At first I'd wanted only to end my life. But I came here, and I started to be who I truly was. I made many mistakes, of course. I don't know much, but what I do know is this — I'm happy now, because I'm being *me,* and not who my poor dear mother wanted to make me."

Beryl was almost in tears now, and becoming only more upset as she went on.

"My mother loved me, and I knew it, which is the one thing that made it so hard. But the hardest and most shameful thing, the thing I live with every day, is that I hated her. I hated her for trying to protect me. And when she died we weren't on speaking terms. Please, Coral. Don't go through that, you and Willie. *Please.*"

And by then, tears were streaming freely down Beryl's face, and she looked so much older than Coral had previously thought her. Then the younger woman consoled the older one, rubbing her forearm with her hands, and they looked into each other's eyes, and Coral said, "I'll try, Beryl. I promise, I'll try."

And Coral noticed that her own eyes were filling with tears, and she knew the road ahead of her would not be easy, for she had, at times, heard that small voice too — and she knew she could no longer ignore it.

18

Everyone made their way back into the church, leaving the main street of Come-By-Chance all but deserted — except for one man, whose job it was to make sure no one interfered with the building materials meant for the new bank; and more than fifty horses, whose job it was to wait patiently so they could cart people back home once they were done with their voting. And their arguing, drinking, good-natured ribbing, and whatever else all those people were about to get up to.

Wally Davis was the last man to enter the church, excited as he was by all these new horses in town, and Roy Black was right there beside him.

"Hurry up, you two," Kate told them, "you can look at all the pretty horses later. It's like having a pair of young children to watch over."

Once everyone was settled, the preacher declared the Town Meeting started, and declared that everyone who lived within twenty miles would be entitled to one vote as to who would become the Mayor.

77

"Even women?" said James Moriarty. "You cannot be serious."

"I vote that Moriarty shuts his mouth or puts up his fists," shouted Penny Carmichael, as her boys Jed and Jethro struggled to hold her back from getting across the room to where Moriarty was standing.

"Sit down, all of you," cried the preacher. "This is still the Lord's House, regardless of whether it's a church service or anything else, and I won't abide fighting. Mister Moriarty, if you'd attended last week's Town Meeting, you'd have been able to vote *against* women being allowed to vote in Come-By-Chance. In which case, you'd have lost, just so you know, twenty-six votes to one. Don't raise the issue again, or I'll have Sheriff Johnson remove you from the meeting."

The Sheriff glared hard at Moriarty, who resumed his seat. He knew he was already on thin ice, having previously had a run-in with Sheriff Johnson's new wife, Opal, just last month.

"We are officially open for nominations for the position of Mayor," said Preacher Coy.

"Penny Carmichael," said Bert Harrison's wife, Sally, and most people looked hard at Moriarty when she said it — but the man only sat there, refusing to bite at the bait.

"Penny," said the preacher, "do you accept?"

"No, I do not. I's too old and ugly to be Mayor," said Penny. "What we need's a right sharp young mind to take the town forward. Someone like Gilbert Milligan, I reckon."

"Is that a nomination?" asked Preacher Ernest Coy.

"If'n that's what you call it," said Penny. "Now let's vote on it!"

"Hold your horses, Penny," said Ernest. "Gilbert hasn't approved his nomination, plus there'll be others before we vote. Gilbert?"

"Oh, yes," Emmy-Lou piped up before Gilbert had a chance to say no. "My Gilbie-Wilbie-Woo shall make a *fine* Mayor, and everyone with *any* sense knows it."

"*No!*" cried Gilbert. "I can't, I'm…"

"You're what?" asked Ben Wilkinson. "Emmy-Lou and Penny are right, Gilbert. I planned to nominate you myself. You're a fine man, you got book-learning *and* commonsense, you showed your bravery plus a cool head when the chips were down, saved the whole town, pretty much. You're our man, Gilbert."

"Yeah," said Matt and Toby Wilkinson together, "you're our man!"

And within seconds, just about all in attendance were speaking all over the top of each other agreeing with Ben that Gilbert Milligan was indeed their man.

Once Ernest Coy managed to quiet them all down

again, he said, "Gilbert? Will you accept the nomination? Please?"

It meant a lot to Gilbert that even the preacher wanted him to say yes, and with a lump in his throat, he said, "Okay then. I accept the nomination, and thank you for it. But I have a better idea — I nominate Sheriff Calvin Johnson. He's the logical choice."

"Thank you, Gilbert," said Calvin, "but I must decline. I have a feeling I'll be busy enough as Sheriff — and besides, I've got my money on you as being the man to take this town forward, just like Penny and Ben and Emmy-Lou said."

"Any further nominations?" asked the preacher. "Anyone?"

A silence came over them all, then after a few seconds, young Henry Miller said, "I nominate Wally Davis's gray horse," and everyone laughed fit to bust.

"I second that nomination," said Toby Wilkinson when they all quieted down. "Why, I won a whole year's good wages when he won the Billings Cup."

"I don't think I can accept the nomination," said the preacher.

"Actually," said Kate Davis, glaring at young Henry as she said it, "as pointless and preposterous as it seems, there's nothing in the minutes from last week's meeting that disallows it. I'm sorry, Preacher, but I do believe you'll have to accept the feebleminded foolishness, then amend the rules before next time."

"Nomination accepted," said Ernest Coy. "Anyone else?"

There were no further nominations, so it was put to a show of hands, and the minutes of the Town Meeting for the first ever voting for Mayor in the town of Come-By-Chance showed that the voting was tallied as fifty-six votes for Gilbert Milligan, four votes for Wally Davis's horse — Gilbert voted for the horse on the grounds that a fair man always votes for his opposition; his parents too voted for the horse as they felt they had to remain more-or-less impartial; and Emmy-Lou voted for the horse because, while Gilbert knew a few tricks of his own, he did not know *quite* so many as the horse, and besides, she was still feeling a mite grouchy with Gilbert on account of the way he had asked her to be quiet earlier.

And while anyone would have thought that Kate Davis had her hands full enough just keeping up with taking the minutes in a general sort of a way, somehow she managed to take them in such a detailed fashion that the records clearly and permanently showed that one asinine, preposterous, muddle-headed, cocka-mamy, grizzled, gray-haired old fossil held both his hands out sideways when votes were called for each candidate — this action, after some discussion, was eventually recorded as half a vote for Gilbert and half a vote for the horse — because one Wallace Erasmus Davis refused point blank to take sides, on account of the both of them meaning so much to him.

19

THERE WAS SOMETHING ABOUT HAVING A GOOD CRY together that brought Beryl and Coral closer than they already had been, but the pair barely had time to dry their eyes before the doorbell rang, and Hattie was opening the door to all manner of cheerful, chattering ladies.

"Do you play an instrument?" Beryl asked Coral, who shook her head. "Neither do I — but that doesn't matter, it's still wonderful fun to take part. Shall we go downstairs and meet the ladies?"

"Why not," said Coral, and the pair descended the stairs to find, much to Coral's amazement, almost twenty women of all shapes, sizes and colors — many of them carrying instruments — all setting themselves up in the grand ballroom around which Beryl's house had been built.

"Welcome, everyone," Beryl called above the noise. "We have a new arrival, Coral — I know you'll all make her welcome."

Coral was overwhelmed then by the hellos and good wishes of all the women, as many of them rushed to greet her, amid a general hullaballoo she had never before been a part of. She shook hands with some of the ladies, exchanged pleasantries with others, some hugged her, and several even kissed her — on both cheeks, no less.

They were, without a doubt, the most *unusual* group of people Coral ever had met. And she would *certainly* never have been brave enough to join such a group — or allow her son anywhere near such remarkably strange folk, for that matter — unless it had happened this way, only coming about by the peculiar turn of events that had led them both here. And she remembered then, just for a moment, to thank the Lord for his part in it.

Before long, just as informally as they had arrived, a few of them started up playing some music, and at intervals, others joined in, then people began to sing, and a very good time was being had by all.

There were tubas and trumpets, violins and mandolins, accordions and flutes and all types of instruments, some of which Coral had not even known existed. The noise itself was terrific, and Coral became so caught up in it, for a short time she completely forgot about Willie, and it was with a start that she saw Hattie carry him into the room.

He was wide-eyed and smiling, squirming to escape Hattie's arms. Yet after he did so, even when Coral tried to pick him up, the boy managed to elude her, and went walking excitedly about the room, taking in the beautiful sights and magnificent sounds, and even joining in — although, instead of words, he sang, "Lala, lalalala, lala, lalalalalala," or at least some variation of it, and nicely in time with the music.

Then, to Coral's complete bafflement and amazement, all the women who'd been singing changed from singing the actual words, and sang right along with Willie, "Lala, lalalala, lala, lalalalalala."

It was the strangest thing she had ever seen, and indeed, she was not just *seeing* this, she realized, but was a *part* of it. And as she watched her beautiful son marvel at the whole scene, and continue to participate in it, she saw that Beryl was right — Willie was truly being his *own* self, and would surely grow to be the best he could become *only* by being allowed to experience life in the way he wanted to.

And in that moment, Coral Mellors determined that she would do her very best not to get in Willie's way, and to put her own insecurities aside — although perhaps not so much when it came to dealing with horses.

20

After almost an hour of music-making, Hattie began to serve afternoon tea, and everyone stopped for some well-earned refreshments.

Willie's time was in great demand, of course. Not only was he as cute as a button to look at, but he had a most adorable way of relating to the ladies, and there was not a one of them who did not find his company a delight.

Coral too was kept busy, it seeming to her that she had met more people here on one day than she had in the past several years — more worthwhile people, to be sure. Chatting with everyone during the afternoon tea, Coral discovered that several of the ladies were indeed serious musicians who played in various bands that performed in the city. However, these Sunday afternoon sessions at Beryl's home were purely for the joy of making music, unfettered by the expectations of others — a way for even the most serious of musicians to let their hair down, so to speak, and shake loose the cobwebs from their day-to-day lives.

Willie was enjoying himself greatly, dragging one of the older ladies around the room by her hand, and Coral found herself deep in conversation with a lovely pair of twins, Ava and Ina.

The pair were identical in looks, even arranging their hair the same way, and their voices sounded just the same too. They were explaining to Coral that it was always easy to tell them apart though, because Ava always wore red, and Ina always wore blue. Coral asked if they weren't sometimes tempted to wear the wrong color, just to play a joke on people, and the pair giggled and looked quickly at each other and back to Coral, then both made a motion as if buttoning their lips, and began to giggle again.

They were from Germany, Ava told Coral, and as such were *expected* to be very serious — but since coming to this country ten years ago, they had become more and more mischievous, and putting on the wrong colored clothes every now and again was something they *might* do — not that they were admitting it, mind.

"So how do I *know* you're really Ava?" asked Coral. "You may just have worn blue today to trick us in fun."

Both girls laughed, and Ava answered, "Oh no, you would know by now. If I was Ina, I'd have made a *dreadful* noise attempting to play the cello."

"Yes," said Ina, "and in my dear sister's hands, my

lovely old violin would have sounded just like some poor cat being strangled. We did it once just for fun, and got in *all* sorts of trouble."

Coral had never before met such *exotic and interesting* people. In fact, she had never met *any* Germans before — but if the others were anything like these two, she would surely like all of them, for Ava and Ina were lovely.

It was while they were laughing about the strangled cat violin noise that Beryl came over to see them, and she was carrying a letter.

"You've met the twins I see, Coral. I'll miss seeing them on Sundays when they eventually leave."

"Leave?" said Coral. "You're leaving?" she asked them.

"Perhaps," said Ina. "But not yet. We shall see. Hmmm. Whatever is in that letter you're holding, mysterious one?"

"Well," said Beryl, "do you mind Coral hearing?"

"Not at all," said Ava.

"We're all friends here," said Ina.

Beryl then went on to explain that it was news, but not good news, not quite yet anyway. "Lettie Wilkinson says that she's still on the lookout for suitable men for you. Thing is, she's made a suggestion I'm not very sure I agree with. Apparently, the sisters who had expressed an interest in marrying the Carmichael brothers stopped writing, and Lettie's correspondence to them has all been returned, marked *No Longer Here, New Address Unknown.*"

"Please do go on," said Ina.

"It sounds promising," said Ava.

"Well," said Beryl, "the Carmichaels are certainly looking for wives, and have said all along they'd prefer to marry sisters, as they'd all be living on one ranch together. I just don't know that..." Beryl's voice trailed off then as she thought about exactly how to say it.

"Well, don't leave us in suspense!" said Ava.

"Yes, what's wrong with them?" asked Ina, and both the twins laughed.

"They're ... well, they're ... oh dear, how do I put this?" Beryl was clearly torn between just coming out with what she thought, and trying to be gentle about it.

Coral was having trouble understanding why these lovely sisters would be considering marriage to anyone they'd not even met. She knew it wasn't her business, but her curiosity was so strong her words just spilled right out of her. "Just say it, Beryl! What is it?"

"They're ... they're nice, I suppose. Good boys, mostly. Their mother's ... ah, lovely. A very strong woman, you might say. One of a kind, to be sure. And the boys are ... hmmm ... hardworking. Decent enough, I suppose. They certainly love their mother *very* much. And they *did* deliver the notorious outlaw Slim Jim Murdoch into the hands of the law. But they're..."

"What *is* it, Beryl?" asked Ava.

"Out with it!" laughed Ina.

"Oh, alright!" cried Beryl. "They're not exactly what you'd call cultured. They wouldn't know a cello from a gravedigger's elbow. They think classical music is an old man and a monkey playing the simplest of organ grinders. Why, the Carmichaels are rougher than treebark, and covered in dirt half the time. They belch in public, occasionally drink too much whiskey and get into fights, they'd gamble on two bugs racing up a wall, and they *even* ride in horse races. There. I said it! There's some wonderful men in Come-By-Chance, and I still think you'd be happy there. But the Carmichaels are—"

"Wonderful," said Ina.

"Perfect," said Ava.

"Awful," said Coral.

"Oh dear, what have I *done?"* said Beryl.

21

WALLY HAD PLANNED TO BRING UP THE BUILDING OF the livery at the Town Meeting. But what with all the excitement of Gilbert winning the vote fifty-six and a half votes to four and a half, then being hoisted up onto Bert Harrison's strong shoulders by the cheering mob, then carried across the street for a celebratory drink at Toby Wilkinson's saloon, there had been no chance to do so.

But at the saloon, Wally worked his way around the room, organizing which men might be available to help build the new livery.

Of course, he could not help but wonder if some of the new arrivals might get time to help. But he knew it was unlikely. They were a specialist crew, he found out from their leader, Emmy-Lou's "Uncle" Maurice, and would be leaving as soon as the bank was done. They had another job to go to, another branch of the bank needing to be built only a hundred and fifty miles away in Livingstone.

"That one'll be bigger and grander than this one here, of course," Maurice told Wally, "but don't worry, the Come-By-Chance one'll be good and solid, and the town'll be proud to have it, we only do quality work. I wish I *could* help you, Wally, but I get the feeling you won't need us. It's a right pretty town, and young Emmy-Lou's done fine by herself to marry Gilbert, I'd warrant."

"He's a fine boy, to be sure. Thinner'n a slice o' bread in an orphanage, and just as popular," Wally said. But then Emmy-Lou came along and jumped right up on Maurice's back, demanding a *horsie ride,* and putting an end to the men's conversation.

"We'll catch up later, Wally," called Maurice as Emmy-Lou rode him out into the street, much to the amusement of most of his crew, who had never seen their tough boss act in such a manner before.

It being a quiet time of year for cattle men, it wasn't long before Wally had nine good men organized to help build the livery the next week. But when he went to the door of the Tea Room to tell Kate, she was nowhere to be seen, so he figured she had gone back across to the church to get some peace and quiet away from the noise. "Might's well have me a whiskey or two to celebrate," Wally said to himself, and walked back inside the saloon then and did so.

The reason Kate was not in the Tea Room was of a personal nature. While both the other Wilkinson brides, Ruby and Lettie, had been able to have children already — twins in Lettie's case — Emily was having no luck. She had spoken of it a few times with Mary Bean, but Mary would only say, always, that *All good things come to those who wait.* Still, while it had only been just under a year she'd been married, Emily could not help but feeling she'd done her fair share of waiting.

Kate did not know just *why,* but she had been noticing lately that the usually cheerful Emily had seemed somewhat melancholy these past weeks. And so, once everything got a little settled after the initial Sunday rush in the Tea Room, Kate had asked Ruby and Lettie to watch over things for a bit while she took Emily out for a walk and a chat.

Kate decided they should walk a ways north of town, out by the river, in the shade of the trees that grew there. It was a pretty spot, and private enough for a talk.

"Emily," she began as they walked. "You've been dispirited, dejected, dismal and downright depressed lately. It's not like you, and I'm worried. Are you okay? You can always tell me, whatever's the matter, you know that."

"Thank you, Kate, but I'm fine. I'm just tired is all."

"Are you sleeping?"

"Yes, well enough. It's just... personal matters, you know."

"No, dear, I don't know. Not until you tell me, at least. Come on, out with it then. What's the problem?"

"It's been a year almost," said Emily. She sat down in the lush grass beside the river and watched a few seconds as some ducks argued over who was getting too close to whom. "You know? A year of marriage, and..."

"Ahhh," said Kate. "Ruby and Lettie have babies already. You've not yet been blessed in that way."

"That's right," Emily said. "And I feel... I don't know, Kate. I have *so* much to be grateful for. But it seems like I'm missing out, and I wonder if maybe... you know?"

"If maybe it won't ever happen?"

"Exactly."

"As you know, dear, I myself was never blessed with children. It broke my heart when my first husband died in the war — he'd have made a wonderful father. And you know, I'll be honest, I cried myself to sleep many a night. But it passes."

"I'm so sorry, Kate."

"Life goes on, dear. There's a lot to be happy for, always. And besides, in your case, a year's nothing, as far as it goes. It could happen any time. Takes some folk years, you know, to have their first — then out they all come, one tumbling after the next, more mouths to feed than ever they'd wished for. It'll be fine, dear, don't you worry about that."

"I feel *terrible* though, Kate. I feel ... oh, I hate to say it. But I feel *jealous* of my dear sisters. And I *should* feel sorry for *you,* never having had any babies at all, but instead, I'm just wicked and selfish and feeling all sorry for myself."

"Oh, Emily, don't be so silly. Of *course* you're jealous, it's natural, I promise. And as for me, I have a *whole* town full of children to mother, at least that's how it feels. Between Henry and Rose and their brood, and Roy and the rest of the Black boys, I'm up to my ears in mothering. And you, dear — you feel like a daughter to me too, and I know Mary Bean feels the same way. So don't worry, you'll be fine. Just one thing..."

"What's that?"

"Is Toby ... you know?" Kate's voice had become a mixture of mysterious and quizzical.

"No," Emily answered. "Whatever do you mean?"

"I mean, is Toby ... you know, crowing as he should be?"

Emily looked puzzled, and said, "I don't quite *follow* what you're saying, Kate."

"You know? Is Toby ... king of his own henhouse? Doing the job as he should be?"

Emily Wilkinson's hands covered her face as it burned a bright crimson, and she squealed, *"Kate! Oh my goodness!"*

"Well, I'm just making sure," Kate said in a matter-of-fact voice. "I've heard stories during *my* life, I'll tell you. A postmistress hears it all, believe me. Sometimes the man doesn't quite learn the right way, as it happens. Does he … you know!"

Emily's hands still covered her face. *"Kate!"* she squealed again.

"No need to be shy, girl, it's all perfectly natural. The Lord didn't build us the way he did without good reason. I'll get Wally to have a quiet word with Toby, make sure he's doing the right—"

"Noooooo," cried Emily. "Kate, *please*. No. I promise, it's not that. *Goodness me, Kate.*"

"I tell you, dear, I don't know where Wally gets the energy at his age, but the man's an absolute tiger. Why, if he can't give Toby some pointers, I'll be very—"

By now, poor Emily had closed her eyes, put her fingers in her ears, and was shaking her head from side to side and saying, *"No no no no no no no no no no no no,"* quite loudly.

Kate waited for her to finish, then when Emily opened an eye to peek out at her again, the older woman smiled and softly said, "You're sure, dear?"

"Yes, Kate, quite sure. I know you mean well, and thank you. But … you know, now I think about it, you were right in the first instance. It's not yet been even a year. I don't know why I've been so impatient. I'm sure we'll be fine."

Emily got up off the grass then, walked to the edge of the river, and cooled her face with some water. Then she burst into laughter, and said, "Thank you, Kate. I'll never be able to look your husband in the eye again, but for some reason, I feel much more cheerful!"

"Any time," Kate Davis told her. "Must just have needed a little color in that pretty face of yours." And they walked slowly back to the Tea Room, hand in hand, and giggled all the way as they went.

22

Beryl Waters had no intention of giving in so easily regarding the Carmichaels. It wasn't that she didn't *like* them — she did. She just believed Ava and Ina better suited to men who were not quite *so* rough in their manner.

"Girls," she began. "I know how romantic it sounds, Jed and Jethro being tough young cowboys and all, but—"

"*Oh, Jed!*" said Ava.

"*Oh, Jethro,*" said Ina.

"*Oh my goodness,*" said Coral.

"*Oh, please listen to reason,*" said Beryl. "Listen, girls. Let's be sensible now. What about the Black boys? There are four of them, good, decent young men, *fine* young men in fact, working together growing crops on a huge farm at Deer Creek, just a few miles downriver from Come-By-Chance. Tough young cowboy *types* like the Carmichaels, but much less wild, you see. The sort of men who'll be gentle with their children, teach them to grow things and make things. Why, you should see the magnificent leather-work Roy does. Art, that's what it is! It puzzles me he's not been snapped up already — but he hasn't. That's why Lettie suggested him for you in her letter, along with *any* of his brothers. All equally fine boys. What do you say?"

"*Jed!*" said Ava.

"*Jethro!*" said Ina.

"An artist and a farmer you say," said Coral quietly, her eyes looking deep into Beryl's. "He sounds ... solid. Dependable. I wonder if ... I mean, it seems silly to even consider it, but ..."

Coral's voice trailed off then, but it was obvious to Beryl that a seed had been sown in the young woman's mind. Whether it was the talk they'd just had upstairs or some other thing entirely, Beryl could not know — but a feeling of the very rightness of it all washed over Beryl Waters the way the sun washes over a late Spring day in Omaha. And she knew for sure it was all meant to be.

"Coral, dear," she said. "I'd not have you rush into it — just as I shan't allow *you other two* to run off and marry the Carmichaels without at least exchanging a few letters beforehand. But Roy *is* a fine young man, and there's another important factor to consider which ... well, perhaps I shouldn't say anything."

Coral was not about to let the conversation rest.

"Please, Beryl. Whatever it is, I'll never repeat it, I promise. And it's Willie's whole life at stake here, after all. If it's pertinent, *please* tell me."

"Yes, all right then. I don't wish to be indelicate, but most men have no interest in raising another man's child — so *you'll* find it more difficult to marry well than the twins here."

"So he *won't* wish to marry me?" Coral said, the disappointment plain in her voice.

"On the contrary, dear. Roy has already showed his quality by agreeing to be paired up with a woman who had a six-year-old. Unfortunately for her, she changed her mind without ever having met him, and married a man from California, I believe. Her loss, I'm certain. Coral, I'd like you to think carefully on it, but yes, Roy Black is a good man, and you're unlikely to find a better one. He won't be available much longer, I guarantee it."

"*We'll go!*" said Coral, a great rush of certainty overtaking her as she said it. "*I'll marry the man if he'll have me.*"

"*And I'll marry Jed!*" said Ava.

"*And I'll marry Jethro!*" said Ina.

"*Whoa, all of you!*" said Beryl. "You two, I'll deal with later. *Wherever* did all this silliness come from? For now, go and ask Hattie to take you to the study, and write letters to the Carmichaels, as you refuse to come to your senses and marry a Black. And Coral, let us discuss this. Yesterday you wanted no man in your life ever again — today, suddenly, you're to run off to Come-By-Chance and *marry* one? You've been through a lot, dear, and I simply *can't* allow you to make such a hurried decision."

The twins went off to the study, giggling and chattering and calling each other *"Mrs Carmichael,"* leaving Coral and Beryl alone.

Coral watched them go, then gazed at Willie a few moments. The child was being danced all about the room by an old Polish woman, his smile seeming almost to light the place up. "Beryl. I know it seems sudden, but you're right, I can't just stop living. I need to move forward, and more importantly, so does Willie. For too long I've been afraid, held him back from living his own life — just look at him now, dancing and smiling. I've never seen him so happy. And Roy Black sounds like the *right* sort of man. *Gentle,* you said. He sounds dependable and caring. I can't keep Willie away from men, but I can make sure he's raised by the right *sort* of man. And it *is* right. I feel it in my very bones. We'll leave tomorrow."

"Coral, no! Write to him first. Wait for his letter. Give yourself time to be sure. A few weeks."

"No, Beryl, I'm certain."

"But Coral, surely—"

"How about this, then? I'll travel to Come-By-Chance to meet him, and if it's not right, I'll return. Will you allow it? I have enough money, and I'll return right away if it doesn't feel right." Then she winked at Beryl and laughed as she said, "I *certainly* won't be staying there to marry a *Carmichael!*"

"Okay then," said Beryl, smiling at the joke. "I'll write you a letter of introduction. Lettie Wilkinson will want a personal letter from *you* too, detailing your age, circumstances, likes and dislikes, the sort of husband you're looking for. She's strict on these things, and won't introduce you to Roy without first reading your letter, even if you're right there in person. Can't argue with her methods, she's done very well for each couple up till now. Anyhow, at worst, you'll meet some lovely people but decide to return anyway — you have a safe place to come back to, Coral, don't ever forget it. You're certainly welcome here, always. So you'll come right back if it doesn't work out. Agreed?"

"Agreed," said Coral, her eyes shining now with a manic anticipation. "Thank you."

23

It was a big week for building in Come-By-Chance, the biggest the town had ever seen.

Not only had TK Waters sent these men to build a bank, but the bank was to have living quarters above it for Gilbert and Emmy-Lou, and such living quarters were planned to be large and luxurious, especially by Come-By-Chance standards.

Added to this, TK had charged his men with building a small jailhouse right next to the bank, and they had brought along no shortage of strong iron bars for the job. TK wanted to make sure that Sheriff Johnson would be able to lock away any such dastardly outlaws as might attempt to rob his bank, and the knowledge that such a jailhouse existed was always a good deterrent to outlaws considering a holdup.

On top of all this, Wally Davis had his own team setting to work on building the livery directly across the road from the bank. Wally had at first drawn up a simple plan with a pencil, but Kate had been less than impressed.

"Twelve smudged lines on a bedraggled, begrimed scrap of paper! That's hardly a plan, you fractious old fool," she had told him. "You've not even drawn your lines straight. What's this over here? Some sort of circular wall?"

"Oh, never mind that one," Wally had said, "I think that might be a coffee stain."

Kate had then set to work and drawn up something resembling a proper plan, all to scale, even liaising with Roy about how big he'd like the windows of his house. And in the end, even Wally had to admit it would be easier to build it, now there was a proper plan to follow.

It was a good design too. Wally had always been one to site his buildings in such a manner as to make the most of whatever weather they might receive. "If you can get the sun inside when it's cool, and keep it out when it's hot," he'd say, all the critters will be happy most of the year, even the two-legged ones."

At the front of the block was the house. It was only small, but there was room to add onto it once Roy commenced to grow his family, which was something that both Kate and Wally assured him would be needed before long.

The very front room of the house, facing the street, would be an over-large room, and initially be used as the saddlery. Kate's plan was for this room to be a sort of a showroom where people might cast an eye over Roy's fine leatherwork, and that there should always be a few saddles, harness of different types, and even chaps, hats, vests and such things to choose from.

"No sense not using the front room to display the finery," she'd said.

"But why so big?" Roy had asked. "It'd take a year to make so many things to fill it, and I'll have horses to attend to."

"Ah, that's the thing," Wally had said then. "When the time comes — and it *will*, soon enough — for Come-By-Chance to have its own stagecoach stop, it'll be the most logical place for it, you see? A good-sized waiting room, inside out of the weather, plenty of room for folks' luggage — and even if they ain't horse folk, they might buy a hat or a coat or a fancy leather wallet or some other such frippery while they're waiting."

Of course, while Roy did greatly enjoy his leatherwork, the place he was most looking forward to spending his time was out the back. The livery itself was to be built out back behind the house, and was already planned out at a good size, to allow for growth.

And so, it was lucky the weather held out all week. There was much hammering and clanging of all types of building materials, and as the week progressed each of the buildings grew steadily upwards and outwards.

At one point there was an argument between the two building crews, an argument which threatened to get bloody, after young Henry Miller took offense at there being so much cussing across the street.

There had been a loud crash, a large wall-frame meant for the bank having fallen and broken to pieces. It had very nearly landed on two men, who, in their anger at those who had failed to secure it, had turned the air almost blue with their cussing.

Well, Henry Miller had never cottoned to cussers. It had always seemed to him that there was never a good enough reason for it, so he walked across the street and told the two men face-to-face, "If you boys don't shut your foul mouths, I got a left fist will fit neatly in one of 'em and a right fist will fit neatly in the other, which I reckon'll shut 'em right fine."

This had, of course, led to more harsh words, some jostling, and other men beginning to join in. Then Preacher Ernest James Coy — a dab hand with a hammer and saw, and the first man Wally had asked to be part of his building crew — called upon them all to "STOP."

Wally Davis himself had been about to let fly with his fists, but the moment Ernest Coy spoke, old Wally said, "Wait up, boys, let the preacher have his say, and *then* we can fight."

"Sounds fair enough to me," said "Uncle" Maurice Carlson, who, like Wally, had been looking forward to getting involved in a bit of a harmless dust-up.

Ernest Coy found it interesting that the two bosses, both being over the age of sixty, had not lined up to fight with each other, but had both picked out the youngest and strongest-looking opponent available to get started on.

As for Ernest himself, he was not only a dab hand with a hammer and saw, but was the finest preacher in the Territory — and part of that was because of the way he could see all sides of a problem, and didn't get himself too hung up on things always being quite perfect.

"Now listen, all you boys," Ernest said. "No punches till I say so, alright? First thing, let's be clear, it was just *ordinary* cussing, and not the sort that takes the Lord's name in vain. That makes a difference. Now, I can see where Henry's coming from, and if there'd been women or children within earshot, he'd be well in his rights to be doing something about it. Truth is, even a preacher like me might have gotten worked up and thrown a punch or two if that was the case."

This served to lighten the mood some, and the visitors then realized what the locals already knew — which was that Preacher Ernest James Coy was at least as much of a man as any of them. And now he had their respect, they waited for him to go on.

"But listen, Henry," he said. "There's no women or children about. And that wall-frame could have killed those two men, so I'm not surprised they were startled. Why, I might well have let such words slip out myself, in their situation. And like I said, while they *were* cusswords, they weren't of the sort that take the Lord's name in vain. So how's about we all let bygones be bygones, and not have to fight about it, and shake hands?"

"Yeah," Henry said, "I guess that's fair enough, as there weren't no children around."

"And the preacher's right," said one of the two men, "I jumped almost outta my skin when it dropped, and the words flew on out without me thinkin' at all."

"Me too," said the other man, and reached out his hand for Henry to shake. "I ain't *never* heard a preacher admit to cussin' before. I guess we can all get along."

"Well, let's all get on back to work then," said Maurice, winking at Wally. "Me and Wally ain't paying all you cussers to stand about admiring each other's good manners."

Then Wally slapped Maurice a hearty one on the shoulder, and everyone went back to work.

24

"It never ceases to amaze what a team of strong men can accomplish, given good weather and fair pay," "Uncle" Maurice Carlson said to Wally Davis.

It was Sunday morning, and the pair were standing in the street, looking first at one side then the other, at what their two crews had built in the course of six days. There was still the finishing touches to be attended to on the bank, and also the facade of the saddlery, but all the hard work was done.

"Yep, Uncle," said Wally, "you're right. And it gives them all confidence in their own abilities too, I reckon. I thought you mighta got finished yesterday even, way you was goin' — but you still got a little to go, I see."

"A few o' the boys were keen to work today, but I couldn't allow it, Wally. Ain't right to work on the Sabbath. Gets the boys' strength back up too, a good rest. Don't suppose you might leave off calling me *Uncle* anytime soon?"

"Shouldn't think so, Uncle. Way your boys have been sayin' it ever since Emmy-Lou greeted you that first day, I don't reckon it'll change anytime soon, no matter whether I stopped or not. It's a mighty fine bank alright. Thought you said it weren't gonna be fancy — I tell you, that there's just about *too* much bank for these parts, in size as well as lavish embellishments."

Maurice cast his eye over it one time and gave a satisfied nod. "TK reckons the fancier the bank appears, the more trusting people become of it. So even though they're mostly of simple construction, he always has us install a fancy pressed metal facade to face the street. Speaking of gilding the lily, those are some mighty big words you come out with at times, Wally. Throws me sometimes when you say them, just so you know. What's that all about anyway?"

"Hazard of marriage, I guess, Uncle. Kate throws them big words around like they's chicken-feed, and I guess they rubs off some. Why, yesterday young Gilbert dropped a piece of lumber on my toe, and without even thinkin', I called him a blunderous butter-fingered bungler. Gets into your system, you see, and you cain't shake it out with any amount o' good sense. Still, Kate's a cracker, and I've never been happier. You married yourself?"

"Tried it once. Turned out the girl I married had tried it three times, in three different states. I only heard that after she'd left, mind. One o' them other fellas turned up looking for her, had a bounty hunter with him. They were too late, she was long gone. Took everything I owned too. Have to admit, the experience turned me off marriage some. Since then, it's been church and building alone that's sustained my spirit."

"Ever think o' settlin' down again? They ain't all like that, Uncle, I promise. Maybe young Lettie Wilkinson could find *you* a mail order bride. It's worked out fine for a few of us. Just wish she'd find one for young Roy soon."

"No, Wally, I think not. I travel too much, building banks and the like, and it wouldn't be fair on a woman. Besides, I'd never be able to learn such big words, I reckon."

The two men were quiet then, each of them taking another long, satisfying look at the buildings they'd gotten up in such a short time.

"Best get along up the street to church before long then," said Wally.

"Yep," said Maurice. But neither man made a move.

They were still standing there five minutes later, admiring the new buildings, when three wagons came rolling up the wide street, all side-by-side. The first carried Ben and Lettie Wilkinson and their twins, the second carried Matt and Ruby Wilkinson and their baby son, and the third carried Bert and Sally Heart.

Bert had helped Wally out with the building a few days, but none of the others had yet seen so much as a single stick of lumber raised there, so their various reactions were hardly surprising.

As they came up close enough for the sound to intrude upon Wally and Maurice's quiet contemplations, the womenfolk could be heard to be offering lively opinions on the appearance of the buildings. They generally agreed that such a fine bank was just what the town needed to get it going ahead, and that it looked more like something from a storybook, or at least from a well-to-do town, than something built out by the Yellowstone River, a half a day's fast ride from the nearest large town.

The men though, as they pulled their wagons to a halt, were quieter, slower to give an opinion. Like Wally and Maurice, the Wilkinson boys gave in to a sort of quiet contemplation, the pair of them rubbing their chins in that same way their own father always had when he did his best thinking — and Wally, Maurice and Bert gave them ample time with their thoughts.

"Looks mighty fine," said Ben, after a time.

"Mighty fine," said Matt.

"All of it," said Ben.

"The bank's a mite fancy to my taste," said Matt, but it'll do the job, I guess, and anyone can see the quality of the build. But that saddlery, that's really got somethin', ain't it, Ben?"

"Sure has," said Ben. "Congratulations to you both, Wally and Maurice. I have to say, I was worried all week about this, even though Bert said it was all going fine. Just not used to so much change, I guess."

"He was beside himself," said Lettie. "Happy *now* though, aren't you, Ben?"

"Yes, Ma'am," said Ben, a smile spreading over his face. "Just what the town needed, I reckon. The jailhouse is suitably small too — I was worried it'd be a big one, and Sheriff Johnson might get carried away and have to import extra outlaws to fill it."

"Ah," said Wally, fanning himself with his hat, "that's the thing, Ben. The jailhouse is more for dissuasion and deterrence, you see, than actually filling up with outlaws."

"What's *determents?*" asked Matt.

"Sounds like something to do with dirt," said Ben.

"Sounds like we're all going to be late for church," said Lettie. "Not wishing to change the subject, boys, but Wally, is Roy in town? I have news for him, a letter. Lovely young girl from Kentucky."

"Just what I was hopin' to hear," said Wally. "He rode on home last night to spend time with his brothers and get his good Sunday duds to wear to church. But he'll be here any minute now, without doubt. You know that boy and church. Ever since his Pa died, and there was no longer someone to stop him attendin', he just cain't get enough of it. Only thing is, you'll have to catch him quick. He's headed home to help out his brothers for a few days with some crops, before he moves into his new home."

"Well, good, good," said Lettie. "The girl's from Seattle, and is willing to travel here as soon as I have a man who'll marry her. She's nineteen, has no children, and loves horses. Perfect for Roy, I should think. But for now, we'd best get to church, it's almost noon. I'll speak to Roy directly after the service."

And with that, the two sixty-something-year-old men, spry as a pair of sixteen-year-old circus-tent tumblers, jumped up onto the back of Ben Wilkinson's buckboard wagon, and procured themselves a ride, thereby saving themselves a hundred yards walk — not out of laziness, mind, but for the sheer pleasure of feeling the wagon's wheels turning underneath them, as the horse pulled it over the ground.

25

CORAL AND WILLIE, TOO, WERE IN A WAGON BEING pulled over the ground, although this one was behind four good horses, not just the one — and while the rumbling of the wheels had the effect of making Willie sleep the sleep of an angel, Coral was taking no enjoyment from it whatsoever.

It had taken some days for she and Beryl to organize all the transportation, and then for Coral and Willie to make the long journey from Omaha, first to Billings, and then on to Come-By-Chance.

At least it was a top quality coach, Beryl had made sure to organize that. But as Coral sat in it now, bouncing along the final piece of rough trail before getting to the smoother path near Come-By-Chance, the young woman could not help but wonder if she hadn't made a mistake.

Thinking back, it seemed a rash decision. *Whatever was I thinking?* she wondered. *I'd found a safe place, good people. Willie liked it there.*

She had the thought that, *perhaps,* some powerful drug had taken hold of her — and then she regretted thinking that way, it seeming to her almost like a blasphemy, and she prayed to the Lord for forgiveness. *No,* she thought, *I'm on this path because I've been blessed. I'm safe, and so's Willie. It's just my dislike of horses that's getting the best of me. Sorry, Lord.*

And then, as if by divine intervention, the road became smoother, the coach ceased to rattle, and she drew back the curtain and looked out the window, only to see a most beautiful scene laid out before her.

To her left was a beautiful meadow, dotted with flowers, and while she could not see them, no shortage of bees. A charming house and equally lovely barn sat dotted in the meadow, just so, as if someone had painted them there. After living in large towns and cities most of her life, this was too pretty a place for it to seem real. There were horses, donkeys, goats and sheep, there were dogs and cats and ducks and geese, there were even peacocks walking about, and all manner of critters, some of which she had never before seen in her life.

She wondered if there might not even be a few monkeys and giraffes hidden away there somewhere, such was the diversity of the creatures she saw, like a scene from the treasured biblical storybook she had owned when she was a child.

She was tempted to wake Willie then, but decided against it. It would take him a minute or two to grumble himself awake, and by then they would be well past this magical place. But she wondered if, perhaps, Roy Black might know whoever owned this scene of wonder, and might even bring them to visit, so Willie could see this sight for himself — without getting too close to the animals, of course.

The nearer Coral had come to her destination, the more nervous about it she was getting. It seemed she had gone from believing herself *Guided by a higher power* before she began the train trip, to *Full of confidence* as the train left the station, to *It will probably work out fine* by the time they arrived in Billings, to *Whatever was I thinking* when the coach started its long journey toward Come-By-Chance the next morning — and until just a minute ago, her mood had gotten progressively worse from there.

But somehow, her little discussion with herself, and apology to the Lord, immediately followed by seeing a place of such rare beauty, was just the tonic she needed. In that moment, Coral Mellors set her mind back once more to being positive about the outcome, and promised herself — and the Lord, too, if he was listening — that she would give her very best to this venture; that she would not be afraid for her own and Willie's future;

and also, that she would meet Roy Black and give him the chance he deserved to be a good husband, if only he would have her.

With these thoughts still uppermost in her mind, Coral Mellors entered the town of Come-By-Chance, and was delivered safely by the coach-driver to where she planned to stay, at the hotel and tea room run by Toby and Emily Wilkinson.

26

CORAL STEPPED OUT OF THE COACH WHEN THE DRIVER opened the door for her, but did not wake Willie, preferring to get her own bearings first. It was a pretty place, but even smaller than she had expected. On the left side of the street, just a barber shop and the Saloon/Tea Room, then two more buildings further along, not quite completed by the look of things. And on the other side, a very nice church, a vacant block then a good-sized store with a sign saying *Milligans & Son's Mercantile* out front of it — before, once again, further along, another not quite complete building. Yes, the town was on the small side, but well tended, and at least, with new buildings going up, it looked like it was going ahead.

But where are the people? she wondered.

There was certainly no shortage of horses, and a good many wagons, in fact the whole street seemed to be full of them. Strangely, two of the horses weren't even tied up, and Coral made sure to watch out for them. Still, they didn't seem to be going anywhere, and just stood in place, as if they were tied like the others.

The coach-driver was having himself a good stretch, so Coral decided to wait for him to finish before asking where everyone was. Then, suddenly, the question did not need to be asked at all, for people were spilling from the church, happily chatting to each other as they walked out into the street, and the small, empty town was now a full and bustling one. *Goodness me, of course,* Coral thought. *I'd completely forgotten it was Sunday.*

Ben Wilkinson and his family were the first residents Coral laid eyes on, and they made for a delightful picture. With Ben carrying one of his baby twins and Lettie carrying the other, and all four dressed up so nicely, they looked like the perfect family coming down the church stairs, the love between them all plain to see. They were chatting amiably to Toby and Emily, then Matt and Ruby were next out and joining in, and it wasn't long before half the town were crossing the street right toward where Coral stood, half hidden from their view by the coach.

Coral had no idea, of course, who was who, but she watched and listened carefully. As they approached, Emily caught up to Lettie and said, "Oh, Lettie, look, isn't that the same coach that brought Emmy-Lou?

Perhaps it's Beryl Waters come to visit, wouldn't that be wonderful!"

Coral pushed a stray strand of hair back under her bonnet and stood herself up half-a-smidgen straighter so as to look less fearful than she felt. Then, plucking up her courage when the group rounded the coach and saw her in front of them, she said, "Excuse me, I couldn't help overhearing. My name is Coral Mellors. If you're Lettie Wilkinson, then it's you I've come to see. Might we speak once you get a few minutes?"

The whole group stopped at once, and Toby, who was bringing up the rear — and having his mind on food as he so often did — walked right into the back of his brother Matt, the pair of them ending up on their behinds on the street, much to the amusement of everyone else.

"Hey, Toby," cried Matt. *"Watch it."*

"You watch it," said Toby. "You can't just stop pedasterin' along for no reason. You's a menace to pedastararian traffic."

"Now what sorta fancy speakin' is *that?*" asked Matt. "You been spendin' too much time with Kate and Wally."

And the pair of them helped each other to their feet, having a good laugh together as they did so, and brushing dust off themselves with their hats.

Ruby's mind went back to the first time she saw Matt. He had tripped over in this very street and ended up smiling at her through a face-full of horse dung. She couldn't help smiling now at the thought, but luckily, she bit her tongue without saying anything. *There's some things you just don't tell strangers,* she thought, *at least not right away.*

"I'm sorry about my brothers," Lettie said to Coral. "They're not half so silly as they first appear. We can talk together in the tea room directly, if it suits you."

Just then, a small but strong voice was heard from nearby. *"Mommy, mommy! Horsies!"*

"I'll collect my son from the coach and meet you inside then?" Coral said to Lettie.

"Wonderful," said Lettie. "We'll have a cup of tea and some pie, you must be famished after your journey."

And with that, the WIlkinsons headed inside, Coral headed for the coach, Wally Davis stopped at the top of the church steps to admire the four magnificent coach horses across the street — and Roy Black, who had been following just a few paces behind, saw what he thought was surely the most beautiful young woman he ever had seen, and walked right into Wally, knocking the older man base over apex down the four stairs.

27

Now, there's some folk believe in *love at first sight,* and there's some folk who call it *a load of old hooey.*

Well, Roy Black, he was a practical sort of a fella. He had seen the way some of his friends had fallen for their wives when first they set eyes upon them, and it never impressed him at all. The truth of it was, he figured them all desperate — or at least highly hopeful — to fall in love, and believed it was this *hopefulness* more than anything else that accounted for the quick development of such strong feelings as had followed.

What Roy Black had not understood, perhaps, is that, while *love at first sight* might be stretching things, there are times in people's lives — people who are otherwise well-balanced and realistic, and would never believe in such crazy, high-falutin' notions — where rational thought leaves them, and is replaced by a kind of *knowing.* And that this *knowing* tricks even the most shy of people into getting started on their way toward having a family.

The other thing Roy never reckoned on was this — when even the most levelheaded of folk become struck by this feeling, it's not just that their intelligence has been overcome by a kind of intuition. It's also that this feeling affects every other part of their logic too, and they begin to see the object of their affection in a way which other people do not.

Well, it's not that Coral Mellors wasn't attractive.

She was. In her way.

However, seen through any *other* man's eyes, Coral would have been around about an *average-looking* sort of a girl, well groomed with soft hair, and perhaps something not quite right about one of her eyes, had they looked at her close enough to notice.

Yet Roy Black saw something different. What he saw when he first looked at Coral was without doubt *the* most beautiful woman who ever set foot in Come-By-Chance — or most likely anywhere else, for that matter.

Luckily for Roy, that same strange effect can work on women too — and in this case, it had.

Coral had gone around to the street side of the coach, as that was the side Willie was trying to climb out of — for he had seen horses, his most favorite thing in the world.

First she persuaded Willie to stop leaning on the door. Then she turned the handle and opened it up, and the boy climbed right into her arms. She'd turned around then to make sure no one was coming, but before she could take her first step to head inside to the tea room, she heard a surprised, *"What in tarnation!"* right across the street, and looked up to see something completely unexpected — there, at the top of the church stairs, was a tall, lean man, clean shaven, neatly dressed in his Sunday best, with a vest of finely tooled black leather over a crisp white shirt — and the man wore a most quizzical look on his face.

My goodness, she thought, for she had been struck with that same sort of irrationality as Roy had a moment before — and when she looked at him she saw a most desirably handsome man — rather than what everyone else saw, which was plain old Roy Black, an ordinary fella with not quite straight teeth and sticky-out ears, but a good enough head of hair to make up for it.

"Wally!" the man cried in a deep voice, the sound of it bringing Coral back to reality. The man looked down at the bottom of the steps, then back up at Coral, then down at the bottom of the steps again, where, Coral finally noticed, was another man, sprawled out flat on his back — but to everyone's immediate relief, the man was commencing to laugh.

The sprawled out man sat right on up, grabbed his hat from where it had fallen beside him, and said,

"Roy Black. I know it was a longer'n normal church service, but you don't need to knock an old man down the stairs to escape the place."

So that's Roy Black, Coral thought. *Goodness me, how truly blessed and fortunate I am,* and she felt a rash of heat rising all through her.

Roy took the steps two at a time and was beside Wally in a second, offering his hand to help the old-timer to his feet. "I'm so sorry, Wally," he said. "I just saw the most... I just..." He looked up then at Coral once more, and Wally Davis's eyes followed the young man's gaze, more or less.

"Ah," said Wally. "I seen it too. No wonder you wasn't watchin' where you was headed. That brown horse is a beaut."

28

IN THE FEW MOMENTS FROM BEFORE WALLY FALLING to when Coral commenced her walk to the tea room, there were certain small interactions taking place between Coral and Roy — but aside from those two themselves, no one but the most inquisitive and perceptive of people would have noticed.

Of course, Joseph Bean, top-notch barber and champion spreader of gossip, was just about one of *the* most inquisitive and perceptive people in the entire Territory — and positioned as he was, right behind Roy at the top of the stairs when it happened, he had a bird's-eye view of the whole incident, and was not too shy to keep a close watch on all the participants.

What Joseph Bean later reported to his wife was, "I seen it, I tell ya. The very moment they fell for each other. It was Wally who took the main fall, o' course, down the steps, but them two's in love, just as sure as eggs comes from hens, or I ain't a barber, I tell ya."

What Mary Bean replied could not entirely be repeated in polite company, but it went something along the lines of Joseph needing to mind his own business for once, and leave all the match-ups to the Lord, or at least to Lettie, as she seemed to be working as His agent, and what would an old barber know about love anyway?

To which Joseph replied that he knew enough to have gotten himself the best dang woman in four Territories, and the pair had then kissed and made up, agreeing to disagree on the matter of whether or not the new girl had any interest in the Black boy.

And while Mary Bean was the finest cook around, and was often enough correct about matters of love, on this occasion she could not have been any more wrong.

What had truly happened, the thing Joseph had seen, was that very moment when Roy and Coral had first laid eyes on each other. Even for Joseph, it was like the heavens had opened, the Lord reaching down with two hands and facing the young lovers toward each other, and playing some almighty musical note that set their hearts to beating in tune.

That was what Joseph Bean saw.

Of course, there was nothing the lovestruck pair could actually do about it right off. Roy saw the girl, lost his whole sense of being to the sight of her for that moment, and walked smack dab into Wally Davis's rear end, knocking the man flying down the Come-By-Chance church stairs.

Coral, for her part, did not at first see the fallen man, her eyes being filled with the most pleasing visage of Roy Black, the sun seemingly only there to highlight his ruggedly handsome features.

Then over the next several seconds, the pair looked, at various times, from Wally to each other, to Wally, to each other, to Wally, to each other again. The nervous smiles that came unbidden to both faces were of such a secret and almost hidden nature that neither was aware they had smiled — and too, each wondered if that small curling of the lips they had noticed from the other party had been real, or just something they'd hoped for.

Such are the beginnings of shy love.

While Coral had seen the whole of Roy, his tall wiry frame, his neat clothes, and his good head of hair, all Roy had seen was the face of an angel — or at least what he figured an angel might look like, not that he'd ever thought about that before. What he had *not* noticed, was that Coral carried a child in her arms.

Maybe that would have changed things, and maybe it wouldn't. But it seems, when people are falling for each other in this way, they mostly only see what they want to anyway — or maybe what they *need* to, if that's a better way to put it.

With differing levels of confidence and belief, in the moment Coral turned her head and walked away to the tea room, she and Roy were left with contrasting impressions.

She doesn't like me, thought Roy. He felt so sad then, he never even heard Wally talking on and on about the beautiful brown horse.

But the truth of the thing was the opposite.

Oh goodness, Coral had thought   for being a woman she had *known* what his look meant — *I'm going to be Mrs Roy Black.*

29

Coral could not have been happier when she walked into the Come-By-Chance Tea Room for the very first time.

She had made the right decision in coming here, she knew that much for sure. Lettie Wilkinson was keeping an eye out for her, and the moment Coral entered, she called her over to a corner table and invited her to sit.

Coral was mildly disappointed that Lettie had chosen a spot near the back of the room, for she would not be able to watch for Roy Black through the window.

"What a beautiful child," Lettie said as Coral placed Willie in a seat then sat herself down. "How old is he?"

"Almost three," said Coral. "Aren't you, Willie?"

"*Pie!*" said Willie, and both women laughed.

"They're so completely *adorable* at that age," Lettie said.

"Yes. But *so* difficult to keep out of things. Your twins are just darling. One of each?"

"Yes, this is Mary," said Lettie, continuing to rock the almost-asleep baby, "and Cleveland's gone off with his daddy to visit Joseph Bean, the barber, next door."

Emily came by then and, after the introductions, took orders from Coral and Lettie — and of course, Willie — for pie and tea. He asked for a whole pie, but it was soon settled that Willie's order was only for a three-year-old's portion of pie, and of course, no tea.

While they waited for their refreshments, the ladies got right down to business. Coral produced two letters, the first from Beryl, the second her own, and gave them to Lettie as she explained why she had come straight to Come-By-Chance without first writing and waiting for a reply.

When she mentioned Roy Black's name, Lettie looked at her strangely. To Coral's eye, it seemed almost a look of alarm.

"I'm sorry, Coral, it's just … perhaps if I quickly read through the letters, then we can talk about who you might be best suited to marry."

"Certainly," said Coral, and while she had seen a look of concern on Lettie's face at the mention of Roy's name, she decided it must be because Lettie preferred to choose the men herself. She would not be accustomed to women who just turned up in Come-By-Chance, such as she had, like a bolt from the blue.

Emily brought the pie and tea while Lettie was reading. The smell was wonderful, and Coral ate one delicious mouthful before she got Willie started in on his. Willie was clearly enjoying it very much indeed, for he did not utter a single word the entire time Lettie was reading, so busy he was with his pie.

"Coral," said Lettie, looking up at the new arrival in earnest. "After reading your letter, I'm not so sure Roy Black's the right man for you. Perhaps one of his brothers would suit you better."

"But I'm certain," said Coral. "I saw him outside just now, while I was getting Willie from the coach. He's the right man, I'm sure of it, Lettie."

"You spoke to Roy?"

"No. Not yet. But I hope to, as soon as I can."

"I don't understand," said Lettie. "Are you even sure it was Roy?"

"Of course. Tall, handsome, well-dressed."

Lettie looked somehow confused. "He *does* dress neatly for church," she said. "But... Coral, how can you be sure you have the right man? I think perhaps you saw the preacher, Ernest Coy."

"No, it was Roy. He knocked an old man down the church stairs, then helped him up. The old man scolded him about it, in a good-natured way, and called him Roy Black."

"Ah, that'll be Wally Davis," said Lettie. "He's become like a father to Roy since … never mind, let's stick to the subject or we'll run out of time. You say in your letter you want a *quiet* man. That's not how I'd describe Roy at all. His brother, Archie, though … now he's just the sort of man that should suit you."

"I can't imagine he'd be nearly so handsome as Roy, or that I'd feel the same way when I saw him. No, Lettie, I'm certain that Roy's the right man."

Lettie was glad that Coral saw Roy as handsome — she would not have used the word herself — but she knew it took much more than that to make a marriage work. She knew from Coral's own letter there were things about Roy that made the pair less than suited, and she cleared her mind for a moment, working out just how to put it.

She was ready to make her case, point by point, using Coral's own letter, about the reasons Roy wasn't the right man at all — but before Lettie could get herself started, Coral spoke up once again.

"Lettie. I know this will sound strange, and makes no sense at all, on the surface. But outside, just now, when I saw Roy for the very first time, I had no idea *who* he was. He walked out of the church, and the shards of sunlight were streaming down upon him, just like it was the Lord's way of pointing him out to me. And that's just how it *felt* too. I don't expect you to understand, but from the moment I heard his name, I've felt like I was *destined* to marry him. And today, just when I'd started to doubt it, I *saw* him, and felt it again. It's him, Lettie. I'm meant to marry Roy Black, I just *know* it."

Thing was, this did *not* sound strange to Lettie Wilkinson, not at all. In the very first moment she had seen Ben, she had felt such a knowing herself — and despite the seemingly impossible circumstances they were in at that time, their love had been written in the stars, that much Lettie now knew.

And Lettie thought then of the last line the wise Beryl Waters had written in her letter, although that part had been referring to the Carmichaels possibly marrying Ava and Ina — *"Perhaps I was wrong,"* Beryl had written. *"Perhaps, sometimes, no matter how incompatible people might seem on the surface, the Lord decides to throw them together, for reasons known only to Himself. For all our own best judgment and application of knowledge, He will always construct such matches in His own way. Sometimes, perhaps, the best we can do is to shake our heads and wonder at His choices, while trusting He knows what he's doing, and try not to get in His way."*

And as it sunk in, Lettie understood that Beryl was right, but that she'd been meant to read it right now, in relation to Coral and Roy. The choice had perhaps already been made without her own input — and the best she could do for them both was allow it to go ahead, or at least to give it the chance.

"Coral," she said. "You stay here and eat your pie. I'll speak to Roy right away, and work out what's to be done."

30

AFTER THE INCIDENT WHERE ROY KNOCKED WALLY down the stairs, Roy's heart and mind commenced having some sort of a race, each trying to outdo the other — but within a few minutes, his mind had started to win it.

You just ain't good enough, he told himself, as he stood in the street beside Wally, who was deep in conversation about the brown horse with its owner.

A girl so beautiful ain't for me, thought poor Roy. *Why would any girl want to marry me, let alone such a fine one?*

Due in most part to the way Roy's wicked Pa, Horace, had treated him most of his life, the young man was quick to judge himself poorly — even now that his father was gone. Wally and Kate had done their level best for Roy and his brothers, and they had made plenty of progress — but whenever Roy found himself having a particularly difficult time, the bad thoughts rained down on top of him. And right now, after seeing the girl turn and walk away as she had, he was having a terrible time of it. He stood there, all caught up in his thoughts, imagining himself having a long and lonely life — and at the end of it, no one would even turn up for his burial in the Come-By-Chance boneyard.

Then, out of nowhere, Roy became aware he was being tapped on the side of his head, and came to his senses from out of his horrible daydream.

"What is it, Wally," he said, shaking his head sideways twice as he looked at the old man.

"I said, we gotta go see Lettie about the bride." Wally shook his own head, wondering what had gotten into the young fella.

"What bride?" asked Roy.

"Oh, Roy," said Wally. "You's been off in your own world thinkin' about horses again, ain't ya? I was meant to tell you before church, but when I arrived so late I never had the time. Lettie's found you a bride, so she reckons."

"Really?" said Roy, his hopes coming back up. *Perhaps that beautiful woman was interested after all.*

"Yup," said Wally. "Nineteen years old, from Seattle. Best part is, she loves horses."

Roy was so happy, he could barely contain his joy. "Well, what are we standin' around here for? Let's go see the girl right away, Wally."

"In Seattle?"

"No. In the tea room," said Roy, commencing to fuss with his hair. "Does my hair look alright, Wally? I don't want it stickin' all up like a peacock's feathers when we go in and see her."

Now, Roy Black was for the most part a sensible and practical man, so Wally Davis was somewhat worried by the strange way Roy was acting. "Roy," he said, "You ain't all liquored up, are you?"

"Course not, Wally. Why would I be? Don't have a comb on you, do you? Oh no, of course you wouldn't, that don't make no sense, does it?"

Wally shook his bald head once again. "Maybe I fell down harder than I thought, but Roy, you's the one ain't makin' no sense, you ain't makin' none at all. What would a girl from Seattle be doin' in the Come-By-Chance Tea Room?"

"I seen her, Wally. When you fell. I was lookin' right at her."

It was just then that Lettie Wilkinson came walking up to the two men and saved them from any further confusion. "Hello, Roy," she said. "I think we need to talk."

"About the girl from Seattle?" said Roy. "I'll marry her, Lettie, if she'll have me."

"Oh dear," said Lettie. "It's become a little more complicated than that."

"I knew it," said Roy. "I told you, Wally, she changed her mind when she saw me."

"I think he's been drinkin' moonshine on the sly, Lettie," said Wally. "I can't get no sense from the boy."

"Have you, Roy?" said Lettie.

"O' course not," said Roy. "You both know I ain't touched a drop since my Pa died. That was *his* favorite thing, not mine! I only ever drank it 'cause he made me."

"Well, there's *somethin'* amiss with him, Lettie," said Wally. "Keeps sayin' the girl from Seattle's in the tea room. Maybe all the stress of it's turned him plumb loco."

"Ohhhh," said Lettie. "I think I understand. Let's all three of us go and sit down, and I'll clear up the misunderstanding."

31

THE THREE MADE THEIR WAY UP THE STEPS AND SAT ON the chairs and table out front of the saloon. Lettie had conducted much of her mail order bride business right here, early on, before she had married Ben Wilkinson, and it brought back some fond memories, to be sure.

She waited for the men to be seated, then began. "Wally, I know I told you that I thought the girl from Seattle was perfect for Roy... but another opportunity has arisen."

"See, Roy, I told you! You's more popular than a prize stallion in early Spring! Well, go on, Lettie," Wally said.

"There's a new arrival in town. Perhaps you saw her, Roy?" Lettie said, as she closely watched the young man's reaction to her words.

The look on Roy Black's face could not have been clearer. It went from worried to excited all the way up to smitten.

"Oh yes, Lettie, I seen her alright. Like I said, I'll marry the girl if she'll have me."

"What in befuddled bewilderment!" cried Wally. "Just hold your horses, boy. You don't know a thing about the girl! And now, you got *two* to choose from."

"He's right, Roy," said Lettie. "We need to discuss certain … complications."

"I already know," said Roy. "I won't change my mind. But we can talk if we must."

"Moonshine," said Wally. "Must be moonshine. I must be losin' my sense o' smell."

"Roy," said Lettie. "Her name is Coral, and she arrived in Come-By-Chance while we were in church. She's lived for some years in Kansas, but just arrived from Omaha. Beryl Waters sent her, with a recommendation — and right or wrong, it's *you,* Roy, that she came here hoping to marry."

"Me?" said Roy. "But … why? Why would anyone want to marry me?"

"Oh, Roy," said Lettie. "Don't sell yourself short, please! You're a fine man, there's many a girl who'd want to marry you."

"See?" Wally said. "I told you so, didn't I? You's in higher demand than ol' *Slowpoke* since he won the Billings Cup! But unlike the horse, you can't marry more than one. You'll have to pick and choose."

"I choose Coral," said Roy. The way he said her name made Lettie smile, it coming out of his mouth so gently and lovingly it was as if he had been married to her for years.

"Now just one misspent minute, son," said Wally. "No sense rushin' in like a lovestruck loon. We need to take a leaf from Sheriff Johnson's book, and examine the facts and the evidence."

"He's right, Roy," said Lettie. "Coral's lovely, but you need to be aware of all the facts before you decide."

"Does she want to marry me or not?" said Roy. "That's all that matters."

"Don't answer him, Lettie," said Wally. "The real question needs answerin' here is, does she like horses or not? That's the main thing that matters."

"She has a child," said Lettie, louder than she'd meant to. "And no, she doesn't like horses, not at all."

"A child?" said Roy.

"Doesn't like horses?" said Wally.

"That's right," said Lettie. "And I won't have the decision made lightly. Are you ready for a child, Roy? Really ready? I know that when..." Lettie paused a moment and looked around to make sure no one was close enough to hear, then lowered her voice anyway before going on. "I know that when we thought Henry didn't want to be married to Rose, you *said* you'd step in to save her. But you told me more recently you'd prefer a woman without children, if possible. The child's almost three, his name's Willie. Did you not see him?"

"No, Ma'am," said Roy.

"Doesn't like horses?" said Wally. "Well, that's it then, ain't it, Roy? *Nutty as a fruitcake!* He'll take the one from Seattle, Lettie. Let's go, Roy."

"No, wait," said Roy. "I…" Wally was already on his feet, but Roy stayed put in his chair.

"You what, Roy," asked Lettie gently.

Roy looked from one to the other, then all around him as if hoping for some help, but it was something he'd have to decide for himself. "I need some time, Lettie."

"I know, Roy."

"Time?" said Wally. "Time? Moonshine, it must be. Did you not *hear,* son? She doesn't like *horses!* And besides, you're about to go into business. You don't have time for a *child* as well as a livery, a saddlery *and* a wife. No, you'll marry the Seattle one, and no more talk about it."

As Lettie watched Roy Black's face then, it went the reverse way to how it had earlier. He sat there with his face sinking, and while he did not say a word, Lettie could see how difficult it was for him. After several seconds, Lettie could bear it no longer, and she said, "Roy. You don't need to decide just yet. The thing is, she may be better suited to one of your brothers."

"No,"

"Yes," said Wally.

"We'll see soon enough," said Lettie. "Wally, with all due respect, this is Roy's decision, not yours."

"But I'm…" Wally's voice trailed off then.

"Roy's a grown man, Wally," Lettie said gently. "You've been like a father to him, we all know that. But he has to decide on this for himself. Roy, all your brothers are on my books too. I'll find good wives for all four of you… and one of you will marry Coral. She came here for *you,* it's true. But she may be better suited to Archie or Marty or Milt. They didn't make it to church today?"

"No, Ma'am," said Roy. "Too busy on the farm right this time o' year, gettin' a crop planted. In fact I promised to help 'em the next few days before I move into my new home above the saddlery."

"Could they spare a few hours?" asked Lettie. "I'd like you all to come to town tomorrow at noon if you can. You can all meet Coral in person, everyone can speak honestly about their wants and needs, and we'll let Coral decide for herself."

"But why, Lettie?" said Roy. "Why'd she come to marry *me,* if she don't like horses? It felt all right, and now it feels all wrong."

Lettie took Roy by the forearm then, good and firm, and looked earnestly into his eyes. "It's nothing personal,

Roy, you mustn't take it badly — it was just a misunderstanding. She thinks you're still a farmer, growing
crops. Beryl didn't know about the new livery. Noon
tomorrow, Roy, at the tea room."

"Yes, Ma'am," said Roy, and he picked up his hat and
stood up to leave. "And thank you, Lettie. I know you're
just tryin' your best for everyone. I'm sorry I got sore."

"That's okay, Roy, it's understandable. It's a difficult
situation. I'll see you tomorrow."

32

ALTHOUGH NO ONE INVOLVED — NOT WALLY, ROY, Lettie or Coral — spoke openly about it, by nightfall most of the townsfolk knew that the new arrival, a woman named Coral, was to marry one of the Black boys the following week.

There was much friendly banter over which one it might be, and each person's argument was based on the little they knew of the puzzle.

Mabel Milligan told her husband that she had heard from Emmy-Lou — who had come out of the tea room just in time to hear it with her own ears — that Coral was going to marry Archie. Emmy-Lou was quite sure of it, even though she had, at the time, been talking to Ruby, who was following on behind her. But then, Ruby was sure it was Milt's name who *she* had heard mentioned.

Toby and Emily Wilkinson both said it didn't matter which one she married, as they were all fine boys, Toby saying how nice it was that there would be another child in the town. Emily just nodded in agreement, then, looking at Toby more thoughtfully than usual, asked him whether he preferred her in her blue dress, her yellow or her green. When he answered that he didn't even *know* she had three different-colored dresses, she told him he was, *"sillier than a kitten in a bowtie, and even less useful,"* then proceeded to storm off to visit with Emmy-Lou, much to Toby's dismay.

Preacher Ernest James Coy had heard about the impending marriage from Penny Carmichael, who was sure it would be Marty, on account of him being so light on his feet that she figured him likely to be the best fighter of the four boys. "Surely the woman would choose the best fighter, given a choice," she'd said to the preacher.

But Ernest had told her, when asked to guess, that he would just allow Coral and Lettie to work it out for themselves, with the Lord's help — although he was later seen to be loitering out front of the tea room, pretending to inspect the wheels of someone's buckboard wagon for damage. The general opinion was that he was only hanging about to give Coral easy access to him for a bit of extra help if she needed it, just in case she'd not yet made her decision on which of the Black brothers to marry.

Mary Bean had heard from Sally Heart, who had heard from her husband Bert, who had heard from Matt

Wilkinson, who had heard from either Jed or Jethro Carmichael, who had heard from somebody, possibly Emily or Lettie or someone else, that it was *definitely* the youngest Black, Milt, who was to be married — and that he and the new girl had been writing each other for months.

The newly married Opal Johnson, hearing all the gossip about town, asked her husband the Sheriff, but he only mumbled a few words about not rushing into anything before collecting enough facts and evidence. He then commenced to smile a particular sort of smile at Opal — she smiled right on back, said something about needing to gather some of her *own* evidence, then the pair jumped up on their horses and headed for home as if it were a race, and the newlyweds were not seen in town for two hours.

Joseph Bean, of course, had seen what he had seen, and was positive it would be Roy, no matter what anyone said.

The only one who offered no opinion at all was James Moriarty. The man sat at the back of the saloon as he so often did, drinking his drink and wishing he could turn his hiding-out-time in Come-By-Chance to his advantage somehow. Moriarty had looked closely at this new girl when he walked out of the church, looked at her the same way he looked at everything — that being, he tried to think up some way he might profit from it. He had looked so closely that he saw the girl had one eye not-quite-right, and it set him to thinking about the strange-eyed Opal Johnson, and the way that dang woman had near got him run out of town — and he *knew,* he just *felt it in his bones,* there was something that Opal was hiding. She was too good a rider and too good a shot, and it seemed to Moriarty that she might be hiding out too.

So with nothing better to do, James Moriarty downed his second drink in a single gulp, grabbed a bottle from Toby Wilkinson for the trip — he noticed that Toby was putting on weight from all the good food he'd been getting — and set out for Billings to find out all he could about Opal.

33

As for Coral herself, well, most of the towns-folk would have been surprised by how little *she* knew then about who she might marry.

At first, she had been most disappointed when she saw Roy ride out of town with a grimace on his face — she had been sure, at first, that the man would have wanted to marry her.

Even when Lettie took Coral across to the church for some privacy, and explained to her that she would have to discuss the whole thing with all four Black men the next day, she had found it difficult to get her head straight about the whole thing. It did not help that Willie kept calling, *"Horsie, Mommy, horsie!,"* every time he saw or heard one go past.

After explaining most of what had been said in her conversation with Wally and Roy, Lettie cleared things up as well as she could for Coral. "Undoubtedly, Roy has genuine feelings for you, for he went against Wally's wishes, and refused to give up the chance to marry you, even when told of your dislike of horses."

Of course, Coral's spirits had lifted when she heard the first part of the statement, but as the latter part of what Lettie was saying reached her ears, Coral's mood sank, the same way a desperate man sinks when he struggles in quicksand.

Horses, she thought. *Why did it have to be horses!* She had not expected this, not at all. "I don't understand, Lettie. Why does it matter whether I like horses? Roy's a farmer. He grows things."

Lettie was careful to break the news gently, but still, she could see it was a shock to poor Coral.

"Coral, there wasn't time to explain it before, as I had to speak to Roy before he left town. But Roy and his brothers, they used to run cattle, some time ago. But they don't any more. More recently, they turned their hand to growing crops, and three of the four much prefer it. Thing is, it never quite suited Roy, and he just wasn't happy with that life … he loves horses, you see, always has. And, well, I'm sorry, Coral, but Roy's about to go into business with Wally and Kate Davis. They've built a livery and saddlery and brand new home for Roy, just up the street. So if you married him … well, you see what I'm saying."

"But … but why did … I see. So that's why you keep

suggesting Roy's brothers as more suitable."

"That's right, Coral. They're good men, all four. But in your letter, you stated you wanted Roy because he's a man who grows things, and ... how did you put it? *Not a cowboy.* Oh, Roy Black has his sensitive side, don't get me wrong. He's like an artist when he tools leather, and he's always thoughtful and decent and caring, Godly too, since he's had the chance to be. But he's a horse man, he is, and he always will be, Coral. You can't *change* that. It's how the Good Lord made him."

"Oh, Lettie, I just don't know." Coral looked around the church. It was cool inside, and she could smell the newness of the lumber it had been built from. The Lord's trees, used in the building of the Lord's house. There was something about that thought that stuck to her, right at the edge of her thinking, but she could not quite get to the meat of it.

Lettie watched the way Coral looked all about her, grasping for meaning in this new sacred place. *It's up to the Lord now,* Lettie thought. *Whatever's meant to happen will happen.*

"Coral," she said softly. "The rooms at the saloon are all full, at least until tomorrow, with the men who've been building the bank. I'd like you to stay with me, at least for tonight. We have a spare room, and we can talk more about all this if you want to. And tomorrow, you'll meet all four brothers together, and you'll know … you'll *know*, I promise you. You'll know then who to marry, for certain. And that choice will be yours."

"Horsie!" said Willie, and this time he tried to run for the door.

"Horsie indeed," said Coral, chasing him down and holding him back by his shirt, before turning to say, "Thank you, Lettie, I hope it gets easier tomorrow."

"It will," said Lettie, "I promise."

34

Roy Black rode on home to his brothers, but he did not tell them of Coral right away.

It was a busy time on the farm, and despite all his brothers' assurances they could do it without him, Roy had felt guilty about leaving them to get the crop planted while he worked with Wally and the other men to build the livery and saddlery in Come-By-Chance. Now, back at home, he changed into his oldest clothes and threw himself into his work.

"Whoa, slow it down, Roy," Milt told him. "Leave some work for the rest of us. How's the building comin' along?"

"Almost done," Roy mumbled. His eyes were already stinging with the sweat that rolled down into them, but all he wanted to do was work harder, and not waste any time talking.

"That's great!" said Milt. "Well done, Roy, I knew you could do it. Crop'll be all planted by nightfall I reckon, so we can all go set our peepers on your new place tomorrow, and maybe get some o' Mary Bean's pie while we're there."

"We'll talk about all that later," said Roy, wiping the sweat from his brow before throwing himself back into the work.

Milt would have enjoyed a good natter with Roy, but the youngster well knew that, once Roy got in a mood like this, there'd be no shaking him away from his work, so he too got back into his rhythm, and settled for talking about it later.

Roy Black had carried a lot of upset and anger about with him, most of his life. It had largely been caused from the way his Pa had treated his Ma, and also his brothers, and himself too, when it came to it. Horace Black had been a cruel man, given to bouts of bad temper, which usually began with mean remarks and often ended in violence. Roy had tried to protect his Ma, and his brothers too, on many occasions, but his father had been too strong, too violent, and always prepared to take things one step further — so for the past few years, Roy had kept his upset and anger inside him.

The only remedy he knew for it was hard work — but today, it seemed like the harder he worked the worse he felt. He thought and thought and thought some more while he worked — and most of what he thought was that it might be for the best anyway, Coral not liking horses. Now that the chips were down and the reality of it could be seen up so close, Roy was beginning to wonder if maybe he wasn't going to turn out just like his father.

He was a rotten Pa, thought Roy as he worked, *and I might well turn out the same way.* Some part of him didn't believe the last part, for Roy had always wanted to have children of his own, and had always told himself he would treat them the way his Ma had treated him and his brothers. But the upset and anger in him took over again, and he told himself — tried to convince himself, more like it — that it was best Coral married one of his brothers, because he would only ruin her child anyway.

By the time the four brothers finished the planting, washed themselves clean and set about making and eating supper, Roy had managed to convince himself he did not wish to marry Coral at all, or especially to be a father to her son — and it was one of the first things he told his brothers as they sat down to eat.

"Boys," he said, "this is important. A young woman has come to town to get married, and—"

"I knew it!" cried Milt. "I told you boys he was actin' so ornery for somethin' important to him. What's the problem, Roy? We'll help."

"Yeah, we'll help you out," said Marty.

"Is she pretty?" asked Archie

"Stop interruptin', all of you," said Roy. "Yes she's pretty! Most beautiful girl I ever saw. But she's got a kid, and I don't need no whippersnapper holdin' me back, I got a new business to run. And besides, she don't like horses. What sorta woman don't like horses? One with no sense at all if'n you ask me."

"Then why are you so worked up?" asked Milt.

"Yea, Roy," said Marty. "You seem mighty upset for a fella who has no interest in—"

"*Enough!*" cried Roy. "Listen, Lettie wants all four of us to come to town tomorrow to meet the girl. Coral's her name, and her son's called Willie. Almost three, Lettie says. So we'll all scrub up and put on our Sunday best, o' course. And you'll all be at the top o' your behavior when you speak to the girl, as she's too good for any of us anyways. But she needs herself a husband, so right or wrong, one o' you boys'll marry her."

35

BEN, LETTIE, CLEVELAND AND MARY WILKINSON HAD company on their wagon on the trip home. Even the babies seemed excited to have Coral and Willie with them, and as for Willie, he was so fascinated to spend time around people smaller than himself, he almost forgot about horses for part of the journey.

They were approaching the bend in the river, where Sheriff Calvin Johnson and his wife Opal had chosen to make their home — a small, ramshackle home it was to begin with, but they were happy with any roof over their head, as long as they had each other — when one of the horses pulled up and held a foot off the ground.

With a concerned look on his face, Ben handed the reins to Lettie, and climbed down to check what was wrong. His fears were unfounded, it being just a small stone giving the horse discomfort, and he quickly worked it out. He was about to climb back up to get moving again when Sheriff Johnson called out to him, "Ben! Everything okay?"

Ben turned to see the sheriff walking toward him, the man looking relaxed and happy indeed. "Howdy, Sheriff," he said. "Married life agreeing with you, I see. It was just a stone. Did you meet Miss Coral yet, and her son Willie?"

"Miss Coral," said Calvin, tipping his hat. "And howdy to you, Willie."

"Hello, Sheriff," Coral said, and Willie just smiled then went back to staring at the babies.

"Sheriff," said Lettie, "I was wondering if… perhaps you and Opal might come for a meal this evening? I meant to ask you in town, but things got too busy."

"Well," said Calvin, "as a man for facts and evidence, I've weighed it all up. Fact is, Opal deserves a night out. And the evidence shows that you, Lettie Wilkinson, are a fine cook, so yes, thank you kindly, we'd be only too pleased to attend. Wild horses couldn't keep us away."

"Horsie," said Willie, and looked at the man, but went back to staring at the babies soon enough.

A few hours later, the Johnsons arrived for supper. When Coral took Willie for a bath, Lettie grabbed the opportunity to speak privately with Opal in the kitchen. "She and Willie have had a most difficult time. I know you can't tell her details of your own past, and I'd never expect you to. But poor Coral's been through a lot, Opal — and it seems like she might let the right man for her go, just because of certain fears she holds."

"Lettie," Opal said, "it sounds important, and she'll be back in a minute or two. We can talk straight, you and I. What is it you need me to do?"

"Your father's a bad man, Opal, and I hope he never finds you. The life you went through, the abuse due to that man, it's a terrible thing. She doesn't know I know, but I trust you of all people to keep a secret. It seems Coral's husband was as bad as your father. He's dead, but the man was a horse thief. Coral's so afraid of her son growing up around horses, for that was what always brought her husband undone. Problem is, the boy loves horses more than anything."

"I understand, Lettie, I do. But how can I help? I don't have any answers."

"Opal, dear, you have more answers than you know. You fell in love with Calvin, but to be with him, you had to go against all your fears. You had to risk everything." Lettie watched Opal closely, saw how attentive she was, knew the girl wanted to help if she could. "And you *did*, Opal, you really did. Why, when I was having my babies, you risked being arrested by him to go and get Mary Bean. It was a brave act, to be sure."

"Anyone would have done the same, Lettie."

"But that's just it, Opal. They wouldn't. Most people let their fears make their choices for them, they hide so they won't get hurt, they don't take chances. Us women are too afraid — not all of us, but most are — and it's strong women like *you* that show us how to stand up for ourselves and be brave. To not allow ourselves to be crippled by our fears."

Opal walked to the door and listened a moment. She heard Coral persuading Willie to dry himself with the towel. "We don't have much time," she said. "And I *want* to help, I do. But I'm still not sure *how* I can do so."

"Just talk to her, Opal. You don't have to reveal your past. But somehow, try to help her understand it's not *horses* that'll ruin her son's life — it's only fear that can do that. Coral thinks that, because her son's father went bad whenever *he* was around horses, that her son will too. She's so afraid he'll turn out bad if he grows up with horses."

"Maybe he will," said Opal matter-of-factly.

Lettie looked at her, quite shocked.

"I'm just being honest," said Opal.

"*You* didn't."

"Didn't what?"

"You didn't turn out *bad*. You turned out *wonderfully*, Opal. You grew up with a truly evil man, and all those years he tried his level best to turn you rotten — yet you're as good and kind and noble a person as I've ever known. Please help her, Opal. Please. I can see this all going wrong, and I don't know what else to do. The happiness of Coral, Willie, and Roy Black too, are at stake."

36

They all sat down to a fine meal, then after it, with Willie gone off to sleep, and Lettie insisting that no guest in her home would be allowed to help with the dishes, Coral found herself left alone with Opal.

When most people looked at Opal's amazing eyes, they were either stunned by their beauty or afraid of the bad luck they believed such opal-like eyes might bring them. But for Coral Mellors, looking into those eyes brought up something else entirely — it was in some way like looking into a mirror.

In Opal's eyes, Coral saw something of the weariness *she* felt, the struggle she had endured, the long and difficult times she had been through. This young woman, the Sheriff's new wife, looked barely nineteen in every other way — but those eyes, they had lived through a lifetime of struggle, and Coral saw it in a moment, and knew that in some way, they were alike.

The two women made small talk for a bit, then out of the blue, Opal said, "Coral, we're very alike in some ways, you and I. Ways that *matter*. And the way I see it, we can pretend not to notice, or we can be honest. Pretending's no way to start a lifelong friendship, now is it? I plan to spend my whole life here, and I think you might too. So let's be honest, shall we? *What are you afraid of?*"

It had been a bold thing to say. They barely knew each other. And again, Coral's first reaction had been fear — fear of being vulnerable, fear of people knowing how she felt, fear of fear itself. But Coral Mellors had been growing stronger by the day, letting go of things a little at a time, surprising herself with a willingness to take chances. And while it seemed almost reckless to be honest about it in this new place, where people might yet prove too quick to judge her, Coral felt compelled to give back as much as she'd just been given.

"Alright, Opal," she said quietly, then took a deep breath and plucked up her courage. "I'll tell you. Willie's father seemed a good man when I met him. I felt … strongly toward him. But I was wrong. *I was wrong.*"

"You're afraid you'll make the wrong choice again?"

"I'm afraid that I already have. I mean, it *feels* right. It never felt *this way* with Willie's father, but it *was* exciting in its own way. And he *seemed* like a good man, he did. But it turned out he wasn't, and I'm afraid Willie will turn out just like him. And I just don't know."

"Yes you do," Opal told her. "I can see it. You *do* know, but you're so afraid of what might go wrong, and you're letting fear win. Let me tell you a story. When I…"

Opal stopped there and smiled a grim smile, then looked down at the ground for a moment, it seeming like she couldn't go on. But she gathered her courage and did so — although she changed the story a little. "When … *someone I used to know* … was growing up, *her* father did everything he could to make her like him. The man was a no-good thief, a gambler, a … the man was a *murderer*, Coral."

Opal choked up as she said it, but knowing she had to do this for Coral, she clenched her fists, cleared her throat, and went right on, only this time, she told the whole truth.

"Coral. We both know that girl was me. My father was not just a horse-thief, he was a murderer. He taught me to shoot to kill. To make people afraid with just a look. To use whatever I had to get the upper hand, in every possible way. He even … he wants me dead, Coral. If he finds me, he'll kill me. Do you understand what I'm saying?"

"You're trusting me with your life, trusting me never to tell anyone, even though you hardly know me."

"Yes. No. Both. It's *more* than that, don't you see,

Coral? So much more. Don't worry so much about Willie. He's a good boy, anyone can see that. He's *not* his father — no more than I am mine. Don't be afraid, Coral. He's Willie — and he'll be Willie, no matter what."

"So you're saying I should marry Roy Black? Even though Willie will be around horses, I should marry Roy, not one of his brothers — that's what you're saying, isn't it?"

"No," Opal said. "That's not what I'm saying at all." And she looked so directly at Coral, looked all the way into her, as intimately as if they had known each other a lifetime. And she lowered her voice then, almost to a whisper, and said, "I'm only saying, you don't need to be so afraid. You just need to be brave enough to be yourself, and let Willie be *himself.* And leave the rest up to the Lord, I guess. This may sound crazy, Coral, but ... do you ever hear a small voice, coming from somewhere inside you?"

"That's not crazy, Opal. Though I wouldn't just say it to anyone ... but yes, I know what you're saying. Sometimes, but I usually doubt it."

Opal took Coral then by the hands, looked right into her with those beautiful, deep eyes that had seen too much of the world, and said, "All I'm saying is, be brave, and listen to *that* voice. The smallest, quietest voice is the one that most matters, and it will never steer you wrong. And whatever you do, I want you to know, I'll always be your friend. Deal?"

"Deal."

And with that, the two women went to search for the others, and Coral was left with plenty to think about that night.

37

Wᴡʜɪʟᴇ ɪᴛ ᴡᴀꜱ ᴛʀᴜᴇ ᴛʜᴀᴛ Wᴀʟʟʏ Dᴀᴠɪꜱ ʜᴀᴅ ʙᴇᴄᴏᴍᴇ like a father to Roy Black in many ways, Wally did not know him the way his brothers did.

During and after supper that night, they took care not to discuss it in front of Roy — but it was obvious to all three that Roy not only saw this girl, Coral, as extra special, but that he was lying to himself about not wanting to marry her.

The more he talked, the more they all knew that Roy already had strong feelings for the girl. By the time they all got to town the next day, they had agreed that, even if the girl would not marry Roy under any circumstances, that none of the three would marry her. Even if she was as *wonderful* and *beautiful* and *special* as Roy said she was.

When they were almost to the tea room, Joseph Bean, who had been watching out for them from his porch, told them that Lettie and Coral — and young Willie too — would meet with them at Roy's new saddlery, and that Wally and Kate had accompanied them there a short while ago. Then when Roy wasn't looking, the barber gave young Milt a strange wink and a smile, and Milt shot one of each right back at him.

The boys thanked Joseph and rode on up the street to the saddlery and tied their horses to the brand new hitching rail out front. There were two horses there already, standing nearby the hitching rail, but these were not tied to anything, for they were Wally and Kate's horses, and were trained to stay right wherever they were told to. The bigger of the pair, a huge gray stallion called Slowpoke, nuzzled Roy as he stood next to him, and got a good stroke of his ears in return.

"Wow," said Marty as he took a good look at Roy's new place, "it looks so … so … it looks so—"

"Beautiful!" said Milt. "The new bank and jail look pretty good too, but your place has somethin' extra about it, I reckon."

"Yup," said Archie. "You and Wally done a fine job, Roy. Can't wait to proper go see the livery out back."

"That can wait," said Roy. "First there's the issue of a marriage to settle. I won't abide any rudeness or bad behavior now, this is no ordinary woman, she's—"

"Special," Marty interrupted. "We know, Roy, you

told us a hundred times already."

"And beautiful, don't forget," said Milt, holding back a laugh.

"Roy's right," said Archie, and winked at the other two while Roy wasn't looking. "Best behavior now, boys."

They walked up onto the porch, then went in through the open front door. There was no one inside the front room, but Wally and Kate had already put some of Roy's leather-goods on display, with prices and everything, real official-like.

Marty whistled through his teeth, and both he and Milt got smiles on their faces that were so wide it looked like it must hurt their cheeks.

Archie, too, had a strange look on his face, but it was more a look of admiration than happiness. "I'm so happy for you, Roy," he said. "I know it's been extra hard for you, and that Pa took things out on you more than the rest of us. You took beatings for us so many times, and it'd be no surprise if you'd never got nowhere in life … but you've done yourself proud, Roy. Congratulations."

Archie reached out then and offered Roy his hand to shake, and the look that passed between them, eldest brother to second-in-line, was something that only those two could ever have understood.

"Now let's go get one o' you boys married off," said Roy. And he opened the door that led to the living quarters behind, determined that, even though he couldn't do so, at least one of his brothers should be happy from marrying the most beautiful woman he'd ever seen.

38

THE BROTHERS WALKED INTO THE LARGE KITCHEN behind the saddlery, but before they could even take in their surroundings, Wally was calling them from upstairs. "Hurry up, you procrastinatin' postponers, don't keep the ladies waitin'."

Roy stood at the bottom and sent them all up the stairs in front of him, each man arriving at the top with his hat in his hands, the first three nodding and mumbling a, "Howdy, Ma'ams," when they got there, then finally Roy appeared behind them. He stared right at Coral as he got to the top of the stairs, and for a moment he could not speak, then Archie turned and dug his elbow into Roy's ribs and whispered, "Well say somethin', Roy."

"Howdy, Lettie," he said, but his eyes were still on Coral. "Howdy, Kate. Wally."

Lettie was used to such behavior from some of the men she'd matched up with brides, although she had rarely seen such a bad case of it. "Roy," she said kindly, "Archie, Marty, Milt. I'd like you all to meet Coral."

The other three did not say a word, only nodding. Then Roy, who was still staring at Coral, finally managed to say, "I'm right pleased to make your acquaintance, Miss Coral. If only... if you were... I hope one of my brothers will be to your liking. They're good boys, all three, and I assure you, you'll be happy whichever one you choose."

"Hello, Roy," Coral said, and the sound of her voice gave him the strangest feeling all through him, like fear and excitement and hunger and a whole lot of things all at once, and he noticed his legs wobble a little. He nodded at her then and tried to stop his face from wobbling too, and he gripped the edge of the table, and didn't know what else to do.

"And this is Willie," Lettie was saying, but the sound of it arrived in Roy's ears sort of slowly and not all at once, because Coral was still looking right at him, and he gripped the table all the harder. Then Coral's eyes went from Roy's, and his eyes followed where her gaze went, down to her son who was on a chair right beside her.

The boy looked up at Roy, a most serious look in his young eyes, then he looked along the line of men, Archie then Marty then Milt. Then he smiled at Wally, before looking back to Roy, and stared right at him awhile. Then, looking as if he had made up his mind about something, Willie climbed down from his seat, crossed the room and reached out his hand for Roy to take it.

No one said a word. Roy felt like he should speak, but he had no idea what to say. And when he took the boy's hand, such feelings of warmth and care flooded over him that he thought he might almost cry, right there in front of Wally and his brothers and Kate and Lettie and Coral.

Then Willie smiled up at Roy and led him across to the window, stood on Roy's boots so he could better see out, looked down at the street below, pointed and said, *"Horsie!"* And the excited way he looked at Roy when he said it was just about the greatest thing Roy had ever seen, and he smiled at the child, then without even thinking about his words, he said, "Yes, son, that's a *fine* horsie."

39

KATE HAD IMMEDIATELY SENSED ROY'S EMBARRASSMENT at calling the boy *son,* and quickly said, "Let's all sit now, shall we? We have pie and tea and coffee from Emily, so let's eat and drink as we talk about things."

They all took their seats, Roy being the last to sit. He looked apologetically at Coral as he placed Willie in his chair beside her, having carried him back across the room to get him to stop looking out at the horses.

Lettie talked some about why they were there, and did her best to put everyone at ease by explaining that Coral may yet decide *not* to marry, and may not even be staying in Come-By-Chance, as she might instead travel back to Omaha to live with Beryl Waters awhile.

"Pardon me, Miss Coral," said Wally, "but why would anyone want to live in Omaha when they could stay here in Come-By-Chance? Especially with such fine boys to choose from. Pardon me, Miss, but you's soundin' a bit loco to me." He had tried his best to say it softly and be nice, but it had come out with a slight edge to his voice, and he couldn't help tacking the last bit on at the end, as he figured anyone who didn't like horses must at least be somewhat untrustworthy.

"Wallace Erasmus Davis!" cried Kate, *"You boorish, barbarous beast!* Apologize immediately!"

"No, no," said Coral, smiling. "Wally's right. Anyone who didn't love Come-By-Chance would indeed be loco. I feel quite blessed to be here, and I truly hope things work out as they're meant to." She stole a look at Roy then, which was noticed by everyone *except* Roy, because he was still staring at Wally, upset at the way he'd been so rude to Coral.

Well, from that moment on, everything happened so fast that poor Roy could barely believe his eyes and his ears. First thing, he thought he heard Milt use a cuss word. It was a mild one, as cuss words went — but nonetheless, it was a word he had never before used in his life.

Next thing Roy saw was Marty wearing his hat at the dinner table, then before he could do anything about any of it, he found himself staring in horror at Archie shoveling a whole slice of pie into his mouth, then not even closing his mouth as he chewed it.

Then Milt belched a loud belch, Marty took Wally's plate right out from under his nose and commenced to eat the man's pie, Archie told Milt that was no way to belch then proceeded to do a better job of it — and not even Kate's loud admonishments were enough to stop Roy's three usually well-behaved brothers from making an absolute fool of him in front of Coral.

The whole thing quickly had just about everyone speaking at once, each of them louder than the next.

Lettie's eyes were wide as she said, "Boys, please, what are you *doing?* They've never been like this, Coral, I promise."

Wally, despite Coral's unexplainable dislike of horses, had decided by now he quite liked her, and he was threatening all three boys with his fists if they didn't start behaving in a way more befitting of them being in the company of a lady.

There were words coming out of Kate that were so long and complicated that not even Coral or Lettie understood them, and, all things considered, that might well have been for the best.

Willie was having a fine time, smiling and laughing for all he was worth — after all, he was a perfectly normal little boy, almost three years of age, and there's nothing such a boy enjoys quite so much as the sound of a jolly good ruckus happening all around him, as long as the whole thing stays good-natured enough, as this particular ruckus was doing.

In fact, the only two not doing any talking were Coral and Roy.

Coral had watched those boys each walk up and into the room, and she had seen and felt nothing particularly special about any of them. In fact, she had noticed they were taking some sort of a set against her — it was nothing in particular, just something about the look in their eyes. It was not nasty, just something guarded, and she had felt no interest in any of the three, at least nothing beyond normal curiosity.

And then Roy had walked in.

She had *felt* him somehow, once again. A loud, fearful voice spoke from inside her, telling her that she must fight against this feeling; that she must use common sense; that she was here to *choose* from these four brothers.

But a smaller voice spoke too, a calm, gentle voice that spoke from somewhere much deeper — and she thought of what Opal had said, and she knew she could trust it. This small voice had not just been a voice, but a laugh — a kind, loving sort of a laugh, but a laugh nonetheless. *You're going to marry Roy Black,* said the voice as it laughed. And she'd known for sure it was true.

Everything since then had only confirmed it — the

way Willie had walked across to Roy, as if *he* was choosing, and taken him to the window, and stood on his boots. Willie was trusting Roy completely. Oh yes, it had *touched* Coral, and the feelings she already had for Roy, strong as they already were, now she knew they would grow into love, and would stay with her always.

When Willie had said, *"Horris,"* as he stood on Roy's boots and looked out of the window, Coral somehow knew it was the Lord's way of telling her something. *Some things are already chosen for us, and some we choose for ourselves. But it's not up to anyone else to get in the way of what someone loves.*

And then Roy had called Willie *son.* His embarrassment about it had been endearing too. The man had no way of knowing Coral wanted him, would always want him, would be happy to spend her life with him and never regret it. Because he was only a man, after all, and men don't *know* such things — not in the way women do.

Then Coral had sat there, trying not to laugh, as all Roy's brothers showed how much they loved him, by pretending they were all badly behaved and not worthy of marriage, so she would choose Roy instead.

And now, as Roy gave up on trying to make everyone behave, and looked at Coral at the far end of the table, he saw from the way she looked at him that none of it mattered; that it was him she had chosen; that indeed, all his worries and his fears and all the tricks he had played on himself were for nothing; for Coral was the most beautiful, the smartest, the loveliest, most caring woman he ever could meet, and she wanted to marry him after all.

40

The news spread like wildfire through the town, and all those who heard it could not have been happier, even all those who had wrongly predicted the outcome.

Only Joseph Bean had been right, but instead of being smug about it, he only assured everyone that it had taken no special skill, and that they'd have gotten it right too if they'd seen what he had.

Yes, the Come-By-Chance townsfolk were mighty pleased by the news. Everyone saw it as an opportunity to do whatever they could for the newly engaged couple, and they all pitched in and helped in some way. Thing was, they saw this, not as work, but as some sort of privilege, and it lifted the whole town's spirits even more.

James Moriarty, on the other hand, had never liked to work, not even for his living. He had been an outlaw, with varying rates of success, from the day he'd left home, kicked out by his father at the age of fourteen.

Moriarty was neither a particularly good fighter nor much of a shot with a gun. He was barely an average horseman, and was not much good at gambling either. Also, he had the sort of a voice that, rather than inspiring people into his confidence so he could take their money by nefarious means, was found to be rather too whiny — and people were instead quick to reject most suggestions he made.

And yet, he had made a tolerably good living from being an outlaw.

The reason was, he was good at one thing. James Moriarty was good at finding things out. He was a good watcher, a good listener, and he always knew how — and where — to ask the right questions, and get information.

With just this one skill, Moriarty had been useful on several occasions to a few different outlaws. He had, at times, found out such things as when a particular stagecoach might be carrying a more precious cargo than usual — and also, just the right place to rob it.

Due to this skill, Moriarty had found himself respected by a big player or two, worked his way into positions of trust, and made some good money for his trouble. Of course, he had never lasted long — even the lowest of outlaws don't like whiners, and Moriarty had been lucky, on at least two occasions, to escape with his life.

The last time, though, he'd escaped with a little bit more. He had seen the writing on the wall, knew the boss disliked him, figured he might end up with a bullet in his head when they robbed the next stagecoach. And so he had left, a thief in the night, with rather more than his fair share of the money.

Moriarty made sure, in the days that followed, he was seen to be headed south. He went to a lot of trouble to be seen down in Austin, then again in San Antonio, before going to just as much trouble *not* to be seen anywhere else after that. It had taken him months to travel west and then north, avoiding every place that mattered, before deciding that Come-By-Chance was a good enough place to lay low for a year or two.

If those Come-By-Chance skunks knew how much money he had, he would get more respect — or at least, that was what he believed. But a man could always do with some more, and he just *knew* there was something about Opal Johnson. So much so, he smelled money whenever he saw her.

And besides, the woman had made a fool of him —
and now it was *personal.*

It hadn't been so difficult to find out what he needed
to. That skunk of a husband of hers, Sheriff Johnson,
had been Sheriff of Billings up until he married her.
Sure, he'd have hidden anything worth knowing, but he
could not control any new information — and besides,
if you knew the right places to ask, you could always
turn up something.

And turn up something he had.

It had been just one thing, but even a sniff of something was enough for Moriarty. In this case, it was the
tattered remains of a WANTED poster, almost buried
underneath others on a noticeboard on the porch outside the Billings Postal Office.

It must have been posted by the new Sheriff, just
after Sheriff Johnson had left the Billings job.

Thing was, these posters came in thick and fast, and
the noticeboard was only big enough to show the most
recent half-dozen, so the poster about Opal was already
buried. But there it was, or a corner of it at least, and
Moriarty unpinned the ones crowding it, and a smile
spread over his face as he read it.

WANTED in INDIANAPOLIS
for the
MURDER
of Francis Ford

OPHELIA TRIGGER

Female, 18 yrs,
5 feet 3 inches (est.),
Fair hair.
Distinctive eyes of blue green and amber.
Wanted Dead or Alive.
Shoot to kill.
Was seen by two witnesses murdering
the man in the street near his home
after a lovers' quarrel.
Heavily armed and dangerous!

There was no mistaking it. With those distinctive opal eyes, the fair hair, the height and the age, the description was right, and so was the timing.

Oh, Ophelia, such a revenge I shall have, thought Moriarty. *I'll be danged. She's a Trigger.*

And while Moriarty knew how dangerous it might be to deal with the infamous Otis Trigger, the plan of what to do worked itself up in his brain, just about faster than a bad man ever reached for a gun. He tore down the poster, folded it up and placed it in his pocket, then laughed when he realized how much money he might make from all this.

What a sweet thing to add to revenge.

41

It was the longest week of Roy Black's life.

And also the most pleasurable. Except, of course, for all that waiting he had to do until Sunday, when he and Coral would finally be married. But even the waiting brought a sort of a pleasure, somehow.

In the meantime, there was plenty to keep them both busy. Although the bulk of the building work was now finished, Roy and Wally, with some help from Henry Miller, and also Roy's brothers when they had time, still had to do the finishing work on the stables. They also had to build furniture for the house — after all, no newly married woman should have to sleep, sit or eat, down on the floor.

Coral, too, had more than enough to keep her busy. With the men who'd built the bank now gone elsewhere, Coral was staying in the town itself, in the best room Toby and Emily Wilkinson had. She was kept mighty busy just getting to know all the townsfolk, there being a seemingly endless stream of them dropping by to be friendly.

She had plenty to do though, as well, not just socialize.

She had to choose fabric from the Milligans' Mercantile and sew curtains for the house — Penny Carmichael was giving her daily lessons in sewing — and she also had to decide where she wanted things set out in the house, not to mention make choices of what she and Willie would wear to the wedding.

Roy kept assuring her it would all go off fine, and that he would help with all that, and sort out Willie's clothes. But Coral was still having trouble trusting in others — not nearly so much as she had been before, but it was taking awhile to break her old habits.

One thing that had changed double-quick was the way Wally Davis thought of Coral. They had met in the middle, was one way of describing it — Wally now understood just why it was that Coral had disliked horses, and could see she wasn't really blaming *horses* at all.

This of course took away any problem he had with the girl. He had not only warmed to her, but had told Roy that he would have been a dang fool to marry the girl from Seattle instead, when Coral was so obviously the number one choice.

As for Coral, she had seen right away that Wally, and Kate too, only had Roy's best interests at heart. And despite all the problems she'd had with family in the past, she had begun to think of Kate and Wally as being like the best extended family she and Willie could ever have. And Roy's brothers too, for that matter — they had all stopped their belching and arguing and food-thieving and wearing of hats at the dinner table, as soon as Coral had called upon them all to be quiet, and announced she was marrying Roy.

And on top of all those things keeping them busy, there was always Willie. What with Coral having come to understand that it was not horses that were really the problem, she was now allowing Willie to be around them a little, and the boy was gleeful whenever he got to go near one.

It was hard to tell who out of Wally and Roy was the happier whenever they took the boy off Coral's hands for an hour, and allowed him to stroke one horse or another, or even — when Coral was not around to get nervous about it — to sit on a horse and be led around some.

"Keep the secret, young fella," Wally would say to the child as he winked at him. Willie would then get the giggles and do his best to wink back, the result being a most waggish and jocular look about him as he screwed up his face, which in turn always set Wally and Roy both to laughing, which made the boy do it all the more.

Their plan was to get the child used to being around

horses, even to the extent of secretly teaching him to ride a little. This way, they could, in a few weeks, show Coral her fears were all completely unfounded.

Sure, she was part-way to being okay with horses, but her fears had been with her so long that they had a deep hold on her — and for Willie to live a normal and contented life, they'd decided, the boy's mother would have to be happy with him riding.

In fact, even Kate had agreed it was the right way to go about things, and so Willie Mellors — soon to be Willie Black — had a daily lesson in riding while Kate or Penny or Ruby or Lettie or Mabel or Mary kept Coral busy.

Around all this work that had to be done, Roy and Coral also found time to court. Roy could have moved in to his new home, but had decided to spend his nights either at Wally and Kate's, or home with his brothers, as it seemed to him that the very best beginning to their new life together would be to all move into their house the same day.

He explained all this to Coral as they sat by the river and watched Willie play, and they talked about a great many other things besides.

Without doubt, the pair saw something in each other that no one else did. And while they resisted the urge for their lips to touch, when Roy told Coral just *why* he had not yet slept in their new house, she felt so irresistibly drawn to him her eyes looked almost as if they would melt, and the both of them felt a longing for each other that started in their minds and went all the way down through their bodies — and in the end, Roy could contain himself no longer, and had to jump up and run, growling like a bear, and he dived into the water fully clothed.

"What *are* you doing, Roy Black?" Coral called to him, as Willie laughed and laughed, and commenced to growl like a bear himself.

"Just quenching the flame of desire," said Roy, standing now in the cold knee-deep water, which dripped from his tight-clinging shirt and the fringe of his hair, the sight of which made Coral want to kiss him all the more.

"Two more days," she said with a smile, "and you'll never have to do anything quite so foolish again."

42

THE WEDDING ITSELF WENT OFF MORE OR LESS WITHOUT a hitch.

Once again, the many beautiful dresses owned by Lettie Wilkinson came in handy — and Ruby, who was something of an expert seamstress, fashioned one of them, with the finest of lacework in the color of ivory, to fit Coral as perfectly as any dress could have.

Coral and Emily had become close during the week, and Emily, who was a dab hand at sewing herself, had made a most beautiful hat to go with the dress, a hat with silken ruffles the color of ripe peaches.

There was almost a problem, in the room upstairs from the saloon, where several of the women were helping the bride to get ready. Coral's extra-long hair could not all be made to fit under the hat, but Emily assured Coral that, in Preacher Coy's opinion, ladies' hair need not be hidden under hats when they married, for it made a fine display of the Lord's Creation. Coral then called for a vote, and all present agreed that it should be left flowing down her back.

As for Willie's clothes, Coral need not have worried, for Roy had been true to his word. What Roy Black couldn't do with leather wasn't worth doing, and while it seemed at first a mite unorthodox, Willie's clothing was an exact match for Roy's — except that, being much smaller, Willie's was all the more cute and endearing. Their outfits were plain black and white, and consisted of new leather trousers, new leather boots, and a new leather vest worn over a crisp white cotton shirt, the shirts having been sewed by Ruby.

She had even added fancy embroidery to the pockets, RB on Roy's, WB on Willie's — telling them that, "Both Black men should have their initials on their shirts."

"Goodness me!" said Coral, when Ruby brought Willie in, having dressed him in an adjacent room. "What a *handsome* young man."

"Give it fifteen years, you'll have to fight off the girls with a stick," Ruby told him, and all present had to agree.

Anyone with a lick o' sense might have expected that, of the two, Roy would have been the most nervous: the first fact being that, unlike Coral, he had not been married before; and the second fact being, men and weddings mix about as well as a goat's milk and orange juice, for men about to be married are just about the most nervous sort of creatures you ever will find.

But as things went, Roy Black, as he waited in the church for his bride to show, was as calm as a Montana moon.

His bride, in stark contrast, was feeling, by that time, like she had not only been drinking that goat's milk and orange juice, but then standing on the backs of two horses as they ran for their lives, pursued up and down a rocky mountain by wolves.

"You'll be fine," Opal told her as they prepared to cross the street to the church.

"I can't do it," said Coral. "Oh my goodness! How can I walk? I can't even feel my feet!"

"You're fine," said Lettie. "We all get nervous. And besides, you've done this before."

"And look how *that* turned out," cried Coral, her eyes growing wider by the second. "No, I'll have to go back to Beryl's."

"Oh, babble, baloney and balderdash!" said Opal, in her best *Kate Davis* voice, *"It's not like you have to marry a fractious featherbrained fool like I did."* This set Lettie and Ruby and Emily off into raucous laughter, and after a moment even Coral was chuckling too.

Before long all four women were falling about with the giggles, each taking a turn at doing Kate's voice, and Wally had — in a nice way of course — been called all manner of things, including a *boneheaded bumbling butterfingers,* a *numbskulled ninnyhammer,* a *muffing muddling mismanager,* a *foolish fatheaded fumbler,* and finally, by Coral, a *friendly, felicitous father-in-law.*

And with that, all Coral's nerves were gone, and she knew it would all be okay. She had friends here, good friends, and family too — and she knew that, whatever challenges she must face, she would never feel alone again.

"He's a good man," said Opal, "and he'll be a wonderful father too, anyone can see that."

"I know," said Coral. "Thank you, all of you. I'm ready."

And with that, they crossed the street, and made their way up the steps of the Come-By-Chance Church. The bride looked beautiful and happy as she walked down the aisle and stood beside her two favorite men in the world, the pair of them wearing identical outfits, not to mention identical smiles. And accompanied by a feeling of rightness and hope and great joy, within just a few minutes, Coral Mellors became Coral Black.

43

It took almost a week for James Moriarty to travel to Indianapolis, but he figured it the only way to best profit from all the information he had gleaned.

He did not go right away to speak with Otis Trigger, but first rented a room, took a bath, and went for a haircut and shave while he had his clothes pressed. In the company of such a powerful man, it was important to present the right image, Moriarty well knew.

It was late afternoon when he went to the gambling house owned by Trigger, ordered a drink, and stood about listening awhile. Within an hour, James Moriarty had worked out who was who, and that, to obtain a private audience with the boss would not be easy.

But the dangerous-looking gunslinger who watched over things at the back of the room was who he must go through, and he did so with all due caution.

He approached the man slowly, one hand holding his drink, the other a cigar, so as to be seen as no threat.

"Mister Sly," said Moriarty, nodding respectfully to

the man. "I was hoping you might help me to speak with Mister Trigger."

"Boss is busy," said Harold Sly, taking an immediate dislike to the stranger.

"Yessir," said Moriarty, then lowering his voice almost to a whisper, "I'm sure that's so. But not too busy for news of his daughter, I'd warrant."

Sly's eyes narrowed. "A man could earn himself all sorts o' trouble making such claims and not backing them up."

Moriarty put down his drink and slowly, carefully, took the WANTED poster from his pocket and unfolded it. "I know where his daughter is," he said, showing the thing to Sly.

Harold Sly did not say a word, only motioning for Moriarty to follow him. Once upstairs, he searched Moriarty for weapons, taking away his gun before knocking on the door to Otis Trigger's private office.

"What is it, Sly?" called Otis Trigger. He knew it was Sly — no one else would have gotten this close to him alive.

"Visitor, Boss. It's about Ophelia."

The door opened, and Moriarty, who was used to dealing with outlaws of all sorts, was struck with a strange kind of fear as Otis Trigger stood in the doorway and stared at him. There was something about the man that made Moriarty, for a long and chilling moment, wish he had not come here. As a shudder ran through him, he wished he had just stayed in Come-By-Chance and minded his business.

"Well, don't just stand there, come in and talk," said Trigger, and made his way back around his desk and sat down. "Stay with us, Sly, you might yet be needed."

"Mister Trigger, sir," Moriarty began, holding his hat in his hands in front of his chest He was not about to sit without being invited. "It's a very great honor to meet you."

"Get on with it, man."

"Yessir, Mister Trigger, sir! I know where your daughter is, you see, and have traveled a long way to see you." He shifted from one foot to the other.

Otis Trigger stood then and stared into Moriarty's eyes, not saying a word, then sat down again and poured two drinks from a bottle — the finest whiskey money could buy. "I sometimes forget my manners, sir. Sit. Let's drink. Then you'll tell me your name, and we'll get down to business. If our business goes well, we'll be friends. If not…"

It was too late to change his mind. Moriarty knew he must tread carefully, but he was used to doing so — and besides, he knew he had more than one piece of information that was worth plenty to Otis Trigger.

After they drank, Moriarty told him his name — or rather *a name.* He was not so stupid as to give his own name away, and Jim Morrison seemed as good a one to use as any.

He told Trigger *when* his daughter had arrived in his town, told him of the girl's exploits in shooting and riding — that was the moment Otis Trigger began to believe that it truly was her — and then Moriarty told him she had married.

"You play a dangerous game, my friend," said Trigger. "I'm sure it was an accident, but you neglected to tell me *where* my daughter is." Harold Sly had stayed on his feet, watching, and his hand hovered over his gun now.

"Begging your pardon, Mister Trigger, but I hoped we might talk business first. You understand, I'm sure. And besides, I've more for you than just your daughter's whereabouts. The chance for us both to get richer."

"Brave or stupid, Morrison! Which one are you?" He fixed Moriarty with his stare once again.

"Neither one, Mister Trigger. I'm just an honest businessman with information that'll make us both richer."

"I can respect that, Jim," Trigger told him. "You look like the sort of man who knows what the *wrong* information will cost him."

"Yessir, I am," said Moriarty, feeling the heat as it rose

through his body. "And I don't take this lightly, sir, I don't. Now here's my proposal."

Moriarty then told Opal's father almost all that he knew, including that she had married a Sheriff. But he told him too, that apart from that one man, where she was living was far from the law, in a tiny town that was just getting going, and that TK Waters had just built a branch of his bank there.

He told Trigger too, "The bank's not yet open, and not yet stocked with money, although gold has recently been found nearby. Many men are flocking to the area and making good finds, and the bank will be the closest available. If you're happy to wait to get back at your daughter for her wrongdoings, I can work with your men to rob the new bank. And of course, to deal with Ophelia in whichever way you think best."

"And what makes you believe it so easy to rob this bank? I know of Waters, and the man's not a fool." And Otis Trigger banged his fist on the table when he said it.

But Moriarty knew that he had him, could see it in the man's eyes. "Ah, that's where you'll need me, sir. The man on the inside, who the townsfolk are used to, and trust. The man with the right information. The man who knows all the schedules. I know who comes to town when, and for what. I know who to trust, who to kill, who and what to stay away from, the best time to strike — and I know how and when to create the right sort of diversion to get the Sheriff out of town. With all that on our side, it'll make the bank easy pickings."

"You really believe I couldn't do it without you?"

"That'd be disrespectful and stupid of me, Mister Trigger. And credit where it's due, I sure couldn't do the job without you, and I'm happy to take the lesser share. But let's just say, it'll go much more smoothly with my help."

"Anything else important I should know?"

"Your daughter married Calvin Johnson, sir, and as much as I hate him, he's too good a Sheriff to be found in such a backwater. But I know how to handle him, you see — and you'll need him out of the way, to get back your daughter *and* rob the bank."

"Johnson, eh? I've kept an eye on his career. Reckon I knew his father years ago. Is he the same Johnson made all those arrests around Billings? Even arrested that Murdoch fella, didn't he? Quite the coup."

"One and the same, sir," said Moriarty, feeling more confident now.

"Thought as much. If there's one thing I can't stand it's an honest lawman. Runs in the family, I guess — there's some men just don't know when to give up and go with what's sensible. But you're not such a man — *are you, Jim?*"

This was the moment where things could go either way, that much Moriarty knew.

"No sir, Mister Trigger," he said. "I'm the agreeable sort, just like you need, sir."

"Good, Morrison, good. Now, let's get down to business."

44

THE FIRST WEEK OF MARRIED LIFE WERE THE BEST DAYS Roy had ever known. Coral, too, was blissfully happy, and it seemed to them both as if life would never turn cruel on them again.

From the moment Preacher Coy pronounced them husband and wife, all the way up to when they took their places in church side by side a week hence, they lived through one-hundred-and-sixty-eight hours of pure bliss.

The livery and saddlery were doing well already, and not only the locals had been bringing in business. A few folk traveling through had stopped in and bought goods as well, including one fella who, marveling at the quality of Roy's leatherwork, had really loosened his pursestrings.

Their days were spent together and apart, the both of them, and Willie too, being kept busy with work and play and visits from friends — although Willie, being so young, was not much help with the work part.

And the nights, well, they were like nothing either Roy or Coral had known could be.

Yes, the nights belonged to the new-married couple alone. The pair even spoke about it a little, for the wonder of it was almost too much to bear, it seeming like the closeness between them was something no other couple must ever have felt.

"It's like God made us just right for each other," Roy would say, as they lay in each other's arms in the early morning stillness, before they got up out of bed.

"Without a doubt," Coral would say, and her eyes would shine when she said it, and they would become even closer before they got up to make breakfast.

In church, a week after their marriage, both Coral and Roy had a certain unmistakeable glow about them, and when the Preacher called upon the congregation to sing, it seemed like their voices were the strongest and clearest of anyone's. It seemed almost as if their union was blessed in some way, even more so than it had been for others.

But later that day it all changed.

Before their marriage, Roy had told Coral he felt it was important that he keep spending an hour or so a day with Willie, for it not only helped the both of them, it was a good break for Coral as well, and she had made the most of it all week. But on this day, Coral had decided to surprise her two men with a visit.

After church, the new little family had all spent time socializing in town awhile, then Coral had said she was a little tired, and might go for an afternoon catnap. Roy had then told Coral he would take Willie with him, and go out to visit Wally and Kate. The Davises had not been at church, although Henry and Rose Miller had said they were mostly fine — it was just that Wally had felt a bit tired, so Kate had stayed home with him too.

"I'll just go check and make sure he's okay," said Roy. "If he needs rest, we'll come right on back. But if not, me and Willie'll stay awhile and learn some big words."

"That's *all* I need," said Coral, "you and Willie talking like Kate and Wally! Have a nice time, my two favorite men, and take care. I'll see you before nightfall, at any rate."

Roy and Willie had gone off on the buckboard, and Coral had gone inside to lie down awhile, but she could not quite seem to nod off, and soon got the idea to go and surprise them, if she got the chance.

She quickly made her way back down the street and, by a stroke of good fortune — or not so good fortune, if you take into account the way the day was going to end — she managed to catch Henry and Rose and their family just as they were leaving.

The Millers lived at the Davis place, in the house everyone had pitched in and built after Wally's original house burned down in a lightning storm. They had needed a place to stay, and it was too much house just for Wally and Kate anyway, the older couple figured. So they'd built two rooms onto the barn and moved in there, and were happier than ever — especially Wally, whose happiness could mostly be measured by how close he was to his horses.

When Coral came running up and caught the Millers just as they were leaving, Henry had tried to talk her out of coming.

"You should get some rest while you can," he told her. "In fact, Ma'am, you look white as a ghost in a snowstorm. A rest might be the best thing for it."

Coral looked a little confused, it seeming to her that Henry was being unfriendly, and Rose sensed it right away. Rose was happier than just about anyone that Coral and Willie were living in Come-By-Chance now, as Willie was close in age to two of her own children, and the addition in numbers made it more likely there'd soon be a schoolteacher in town.

"Nonsense, Henry," Rose said. "Don't listen to him, Coral, it was him who told Wally to stay home and rest today too. Always worrying everyone's sick ... why, you look perfectly fine to me. Jump on up and let's get going, I'm sure it'll be a lovely surprise for everyone to see you."

"Yep, a *lovely* surprise," said Henry quietly. For he was in on a secret — young Willie was, at this very moment, being taught to sit a horse. And while no one was *really* doing anything *wrong,* Henry had a suspicion it might all yet turn out badly.

45

THE TRIP FROM TOWN TO THE DAVIS/MILLER PLACE was just about the slowest anyone ever took. Rose twice asked Henry why they were going so slowly, but he only mumbled something about it being a nice day to "meander and look at the scenery," and pointed out some rather attractive bird, or a pretty field of flowers, and Rose turned back to Coral, shaking her head both times, and said, *"Men!"*

Henry Miller did his level best to warn Wally, Kate and Roy that something was up, and his plan was a good one, but it failed to come off. He commenced to sing Yankee Doodle at the top of his voice as they came within earshot, thinking he would be able to change the words as a warning of Coral's approach.

But Rose immediately put a stop to it, telling poor Henry to, "Cease that awful caterwauling at once, Henry Miller, you'll scare the horses half to death!"

It was a lucky thing for everyone's ears, for Henry — although an agreeable and likable fellow — had a singing voice that sounded like a sheep being mauled by a mountain lion, then the whole noise being somehow pushed out through a trumpet.

And so it happened that, as the Miller family and their guest came over the rise and attained a full view of the Davis/Miller place, the sight Coral saw was that of Kate calmly standing by, while Roy walked along one side and Wally the other side of the huge gray horse, Jake, otherwise known as Slowpoke, winner of the Billings Cup, and the finest horse in the Territory.

Neither man was touching the horse, only walking along right beside him, and there, up on Slowpoke's back, on a tiny and specially made saddle, holding onto the reins just as if he had been born to do so, was young Willie Black — and the child's mother, just as Henry Miller had feared, very nearly fainted dead away.

But instead she let fly with the highest-pitched scream ever let loose in Montana.

Such a noise, wailing out into the world as it did, might, in other circumstances, have proven disastrous. Most horses, upon hearing such a fearsome and ear-splitting noise, would have bolted, or at least reared right up on the spot. But Jake, otherwise known as Slowpoke — the only horse ever to run for Mayor in the entire history of the Montana Territory — did nothing of the sort.

For the fact was, he had been trained by Wally Davis, and knew there was nothing to fear.

The boy on the horse, though, had not yet been trained, at least not quite so much as the horse. Hearing his mother's scream, young Willie Black flinched and almost forgot where he was. If not for Wally's calm and quick thinking, the boy might well have taken a tumble.

Roy was less help than *he* might have been, his eyes having gone wide at the shock of Coral's scream, and his boots having planted themselves in place as he instinctively reached out to save the child if he fell.

"Slow him down ... and ... stop," was all Wally said though, in a measured, even voice, as if nothing had happened at all.

Then, Willie Black — who had been taught only good habits thus far — reined the horse in with a gentle lift of the reins, and the winner of the Billings Cup stopped as still as a statue, and waited there quieter than a gunfighter all out of bullets.

The Millers too, had stopped, right there on the trail, just out front of the Davis farm. They were all about as still as a frozen lake in midwinter — the Millers, their wagon, their horses, and their guest, Coral Black, the lot of them quiet now, Coral's scream having run out of air — and it seemed to everyone like something must surely soon happen.

It was Wally who made it happen, of course. "Have him walk on, Willie," he said.

The child shook the reins lightly, made a clicking sound with his mouth, and commenced to ride the horse forward once more, much to the surprise of almost everyone watching.

Roy got himself moving right enough — it was that or risk being seen not to be doing his job — and the four of them, Willie and Slowpoke, Wally and Roy, made their way at a slow walk up to the front fence. And when they arrived there, just a few yards from where Coral sat on the wagon, Wally once more directed the child to stop the horse, and he did so without any fuss.

46

WHILE HER INITIAL REACTION HAD BEEN TO PANIC,
Coral Black could scarcely have been more impressed
by what she had then seen.

It was clear to her that Roy and Willie had been
keeping a secret from her — for the child had surely
not learned to sit a horse so well in just the last hour.
But she could see right away how capable he was, and
how much care was being taken to keep him safe, and
that Wally and Roy knew exactly what they were doing.

And she saw something else, too.

The smile Willie wore was so full of joy that it lifted
not only Coral's heart, but the hearts of everyone who
could see it. It was a smile that was not only limited
to his mouth, but spread out all over his face and all
through his body somehow, but most of all, that smile
could be seen in his eyes.

Willie Black was right where he belonged, and that
still, small voice that Coral had recently become so

happy to listen to, told her so.

She did not make a fuss, much to the surprise of Roy in particular, although she drew the line at taking up Wally's offer of being taught to ride herself.

The Blacks stayed another hour before heading home, the discussion being lively and good-natured, and there was no clue at all of the pain and turmoil that would follow.

It was later that evening when it happened. Willie had been put to bed, both Roy and Coral having kissed the child goodnight on his forehead, and he was dreaming of horses, as always. Roy and Coral had only just climbed into their bed, and Coral snuggled her warm body up against Roy's, nestling into his chest and shoulder in a way he found most pleasurable.

He was so overcome with all the love he felt for her, he said, "Coral, my love. I'm not much for words, and might forget to tell you sometimes, but I want you to know, I am so grateful to have you and Willie in my life. I... I love you, Coral, I do. Just so's you know, and don't ever doubt it a minute."

"Oh, Roy," she said. "I guess we're neither of us the type to say it much, but I love you too. You know that, don't you?"

"Yes, Mrs Black, I surely do," he said, his hand

stroking her hair as he felt her heart beat against his, and that wonderful nervous feeling started building inside him, that special way it did every night.

Coral went to kiss him then, but Roy had been thinking, and had to get out what he needed to say.

"Coral. Please wait a moment, this is important. I know I shoulda told you we was teachin' Willie to ride. And I felt a bit wrong about it, I did. But when Kate said it was the best way, I went along with it. She's a wise woman, I reckon, and not because of big words. I greatly respect her. But I want you to know, I'll never hide anything from you again."

"It's okay, Roy," she told him, snuggling against him once more. "Kate was right, and it was better I didn't know to start with. I'd have been a bundle of nerves. It could scarcely have worked out as well as it did. I know you didn't like having to work things that way, and I trust you. No more secrets between us, agreed?"

"Yes, Ma'am," said Roy. "Oh, I'm *real* proud of him, Coral, aren't you? Sure, Slowpoke's the perfect horse, and better behaved than a stuffed owl — but I never saw a young'un sit a horse near so well, and that's the God's honest truth. That boy's a natural, and he loves horses just about more than me and Wally. Thank you for understandin', Coral. And for trustin' me to look after your ... for trustin' me to look after *our* son."

"Oh, Roy. You make me so happy. And yes, he is *our* son, isn't he? I know you'd never do anything to hurt him. Although the very moment I saw him on that horse — oh, goodness, that horse is a *giant!* And yet so placid. Not a mean bone in his body."

"Well, I wouldn't quite put it that way," said Roy.

Problem was, Roy was so relaxed, all filled with love as he was, that the words had come out without him thinking. Something gnawed at him right away to stop though, and he did not know quite what to say next, and went completely silent thereafter, which made it seem worse.

Coral sat up beside him. Not alarmed, but less than relaxed — and it seemed to Roy like the calm before a storm had been broken by a quiet distant thunder.

"Roy ... how *would* you put it?"

He had to think fast, but so sleepy and love-drunk he was, he wasn't up to the task. "I just ... I didn't mean nothin' by it, Coral. It's just, you know, we should always look out for horses, at least ... that is to say ... it's nothin' at all, Coral, honest."

"Honest?" she said, and the word had quite the edge to it.

Given the way they had both just a minute before pledged complete honesty forever, Coral knew she had only to wait, and the rest of the truth — whatever it was — would surely come tumbling out.

Roy withstood it for several seconds, but that silence grew louder and louder, and before long he could stand it no more.

"Alright!" he said. "The horse ... it wasn't *his* fault, and not Wally's either, I promise It's just ... that horse is protective, that's all, and my father once owned him, and there's always good reasons for things when they happen, there is."

"Roy Black," said Coral. "Get to the point. Right now." She was no longer soft, but a solid presence in the room, and her voice had an edge that hurt him somehow.

"My father was a cruel man, Coral, you have to understand that. He used to *beat* that horse, same as he always beat my Ma and my brothers. A *cruel* man, that's what he was."

Roy was clearly shaken by what he was saying, and while Coral's heart was breaking for Roy and the pain in his voice, she could tell there was something else coming, something Roy did not want to say — and she would not give in and hold him again until he had said it.

"What happened, Roy?" she said. "It's okay, Roy, I love you, you know that. You can tell me anything at all. Just tell me what happened."

But of all the things Coral thought he might say, she

could not have been prepared for the thing Roy *did* say, and the words went through her like a bullet.

"The horse, Jake. Slowpoke. He was just protectin' Wally, that's all. *That's* the only reason he killed my father."

47

Coral did not scream, as she had when she saw Willie on the horse.

There wasn't nearly enough moonlight to see by — yet somehow, the way Roy would always remember it, he clearly saw the horror on Coral's face, then the disappointment, and finally the fury.

She did not yell. He reached for her hand, felt the rage that simmered inside her, the way she shook with it, and all he could think of was that, somehow, he must find a way to calm her — but that was not going to happen.

She reeled away from his touch, her trust in him gone, her trust in *everything* all dried up for the moment.

And then she spoke.

"You put my son on a horse — not just *any* horse, but a *killer!*"

"It's not like—"

"Do not speak, Roy Black. No more. How could you? How could you?"

"I only—"

"I said, don't speak. Please, don't speak again. I'll be leaving, of course. I'm sorry, but there's no other way."

She looked away from him then, and only sat there, stiller than death.

Her pain was a terrible thing. It occurred to her that her first husband would have hit her by now, but she knew Roy would not do so . . . and somehow, that made it all the more difficult.

"Oh, Coral, please," said Roy quietly after some time passed — but he did not dare touch her, did not dare raise his voice, did not dare even breathe.

"I'm sorry, Roy. There's no getting past this. I'll leave tomorrow, if I can find someone to take me."

"Please," he whispered, his voice breaking as tears streamed down his face. "You just have to let me explain — it's not *what* happened, but *why.*"

"*Why?*" she cried. "*Why?* There is no possible *why* that can make a difference. You *knew* that horse was a killer, and you put my *son* on his back. You . . . Wally Davis . . . Kate too — you all conspired to put my son in danger! There is *no reason good enough.* Willie and I will be leaving."

"But Coral! Willie's *happy!* He's *so* happy. And so are *we!*"

"It was all a lie, wasn't it? Everything. Verna was right,

and I should have listened. Oh, what have I done? What if Beryl won't take us back! Oh, Roy, *how* could you do this? The horse killed *your own father!*"

Roy Black just sat there. It was a quiet night, but in his head was a roaring the like of which he had never known before. Try as he might, he could not stop the terrible thoughts and bad memories that flooded in on him now. The harder he tried to work out what to do, the less chance he had to think clearly.

In his mind's eye, Roy Black saw his dear mother, cowering under his father's blows, pleading for mercy. His brothers, each in turn, trying to scuttle away from the evil man's flying fists and boots — and the way those fists and boots had been aimed at his own head, every time he put himself in front of them, trying to protect those he loved. And the horse, too — he had not been called Slowpoke back then, or Jake, or anything else. Roy's father Horace had bought the horse for a bargain, and never even named him. He had done his best to break that fine animal's spirit, before Wally Davis had seen him beating the gray horse, and right away offered the evil man top dollar for him, in order to save the animal.

Yes, Horace Black had deserved to die, and Coral did not understand, did not understand it at all.

"Coral, please, let me speak."

"You can speak. But you won't change my mind, Roy. It's over. I can't allow my son to ever be placed in such danger again."

Roy sighed the loudest, longest sigh of his life, and felt himself shake as he did so. "Coral. He was never in danger. You saw for yourself how the horse is. Why, he'd no more harm Willie than you would."

"How dare you!" cried Coral, but Roy interrupted right away.

"It's my turn to speak," he said, and he noticed he sounded much calmer than he felt. Then Coral went quiet, allowing Roy to go on. "I love you, Coral. And Willie too. I could no more harm him than you could, and I hope that, in time, you'll see that it's so."

"There is no more time," said Coral. "I told you, I'm leaving. I won't stay—"

"I know what you said. But you have a life here now. You have friends, and so does Willie. You can't just take him away from the Miller children now, and Lettie and Ruby's babies, and all the grownups who care for him. And you too, Coral. You too. You're close with Opal, and with Emily and Ruby and Lettie. Mary Bean as well. And Kate, o' course."

"Kate lied to me. Not directly, but she lied by omission She was part of your scheme, she *knew* that horse was a killer. I shan't speak to her ever again."

"It ain't right, Coral, to blame Kate. It's all on me. It was my choice alone to keep it a secret."

"She went along with it, Roy. But none of it matters, I've no way of staying, I'll have to—"

"Coral, please, let me finish. You keep calling Slow-poke a killer, but he ain't. Still, I understand where you're comin' from. But it's all on me — I'm the only one done wrong here. So this is how things'll be. I'll be headin' out now to bed down in the stables, and that's where I'll live from now on. I'll keep to myself and won't bother you again. And... and I won't go near young Willie neither," he said, and his voice cracked up bad when he said it.

"I can't do that, Roy, it wouldn't be fair to you. This is *your* town."

He got out of the bed then, and commenced to pace up and down the room, passing by the window again and again as he spoke, but still, he did not raise his voice. "You *can* do it, Coral. And you will. Please. I'll stay well away, I'll work out the back in the livery. I'll live out there too, and make my own meals and all. You'll need to sell the goods from the saddlery is all — but you can just leave me a note on what to make when things sell, and I'll drop it at your back door when it's done. You can live in Come-By-Chance and have a good life, you and Willie both, and I'll provide for you proper-like — but I'll never bother either of you again."

"That's unfair to you, Roy. I can't."

The small voice kept telling her what a good man he was, but she had no time for small voices now.

"Yes you can, Coral, you *can*. We both know it's for the best. And I never was much for bein' sociable with people anyways. Anyone wants to visit, they'll find me out back, and I'll sometimes go visit the Davises, and my brothers o' course. It won't be so much different to how things were before you came, exceptin' ... exceptin' for the nice memories I'll have. Please, Coral. Just think about it, and give it a try for a week. Just a *week*. If you still want to go after that, I won't stand in your way. Please. For Willie's sake, if not your own."

Coral did not make a sound for more than a minute, and Roy quietly prayed she might stay. Then she said, "It won't work, anyone can see that. But I married you, Roy. I owe you something, so I'll try. I'll give it two weeks. But you must promise to leave me be. At the first sign of violence or drunkenness, I'll leave."

"Thank you, Coral," said Roy. "I give you my word, you'll never get trouble from me."

And he picked up his clothes and walked out of the house to the stables.

48

It was a far from ideal situation, but Coral knew Roy had been right. She had grown to feel she belonged here, and more important, Willie was happy.

As much as she tried not to, as much as she reminded herself that he had done the wrong thing by her son, she still loved Roy, and she could not deny it, at least to herself. She saw him, of course — not a lot, but a little. She would catch herself looking out the top floor window, down at the stables where she could hear him working, and of course, she secretly wished she could see him.

She longed for him at night, cried herself to sleep even. But she would not give in. None of the townsfolk knew quite how to deal with the problem, but it was generally believed that it would be temporary. They were mostly of the belief that things have a way of working out, at least if you have enough faith.

Even Preacher Coy decided not to stick his nose in,

at least in the short term. He figured they would find a solution soon enough, and that if they didn't, the Lord would intervene if he had to.

Opinions were divided on whether or not Roy had done anything wrong. No one was keen to lay blame on either party, it seeming like both were in the right, more or less. There were rumors that Coral would leave in a week, or maybe a month. Mostly, the whole thing was too sad for anyone to speak of very much.

Opal tried, of course, to speak to her friend. She would not take no for an answer, and told Coral that if they were going to stay friends their whole lives, they would need to be honest with each other. Also, that if she was to be completely honest, Opal believed the child had not been in danger at all, and that Roy, Kate and Wally had done nothing wrong — and lastly, that Coral would never be happy until she forgave them, and invited Roy back into their home, so they could get on with their marriage as they should be.

The small voice inside Coral began to agree with Opal — but Coral had lost faith somehow, and refused to listen to her friend *or* the small voice, so in the end, nothing was changed.

Nothing except Willie, that is.

The child had been so happy before — but now,

he not only missed horses, he missed Roy as well. He would grizzle, of course, and beg for Coral to let him see Roy, and once or twice got himself highly excited when he caught sight of Roy out the window. But still, Coral stuck to her guns, and refused to budge from what she'd decided.

A week had now passed, and it was the Sabbath. One week of waiting, one week of blissful marriage, one week of being torn apart. That had been all the time that had passed.

It had been decided, and a message passed on, that Roy should sit up front during church, and that Coral and Willie would come in just as the service began, and sit up the back, right across from the Wilkinsons.

It was a natural enough place for Coral to sit anyway, as Calvin and Opal Johnson had taken to sitting up the back too — and of all the friends Coral had made, it was Opal she felt the closest to, whether she listened to her or not.

Most people predicted that the Preacher would speak on some particular thing that might help Roy and Coral back together — but Ernest was a smart man, and knew not to say anything that might cause embarrassment or upset to anyone. Instead he spoke of how happy he was to see such a good turnout, and how well the town was going ahead, and reminded everyone to be kind to strangers as well as folk they knew.

Then he got everyone singing, it being his belief that having the townsfolk sing together fosters town spirit, and makes everyone happier with each other. Although, he was none too sure if all that applied to Henry Miller, the young fella having such a voice as would even upset those buried in the boneyard out back.

49

James Moriarty had not enjoyed the trip back to Come-By-Chance, not even a little. The travel itself was unpleasant enough, but Dan Donnelly, the man Otis Trigger had sent back with Moriarty, had a grossly inflated opinion of himself, and was annoying to say the least.

By the time they arrived in Billings, Moriarty had already decided the man was disrespectful, disagreeable, and downright dangerous, even by outlaw standards.

Donnelly was fast on the draw, and had made a name for himself in the South, being known as a man with no fear, and prepared to do anything he got paid to. Otis Trigger had brought him to Indianapolis just two weeks previous, and he had high hopes of becoming Trigger's right hand man.

He had gotten drunk the night before in Billings, and said enough for Moriarty to realize that Otis Trigger would be relying on *him,* and not Moriarty, when it came time to rob the bank — and in fact, Moriarty had begun to wonder about his own chances of survival once the bank job was done. He just had that feeling again…

Still, there was little Moriarty could do. Donnelly was no pretender, he was a gunfighter alright, and had showed off his ability along the way, getting in some practice while Moriarty watered the horses. Moriarty himself could not even reliably shoot straight, his hand having always proved itself unsteady when the chips were down.

And so, when the pair came near to Come-By-Chance and Donnelly demanded they head right on into town for a look, Moriarty — or Morrison, as Donnelly knew him — was in no position to argue, and quickly gave in.

"They'll all be in church at this time," Moriarty said as they approached the town. "If we're quick, we can get in and out without you being seen."

"Suits me fine," the gunman told him. "But surely not *everyone* goes to church? What about the men in the saloon? Won't they see us?"

"Strange rules here," said Moriarty. "No one gets a drink on the Sabbath until *after* they attend church — and even then, just two drinks per man."

"So they're *all* in church?" said Donnelly, like it was the strangest thing he'd heard in all his days.

"Yessir," Moriarty said. "Still, we'll have to tie the horses up here and walk if we don't wish to be heard.

It's but two hundred yards walk, and I'll show you the layout of the town and the bank, then we'll get out before the church service is done."

The two men tied their horses to trees, where they could graze on the sweet grass by the river — Wally Davis still would not have been happy, for they did not give them a drink — and walked the short distance in no time flat.

"That's the barber's house up ahead on the left," said Moriarty. "He's never no trouble, except for bein' a gossip. Then after that is the saloon. The other side's the church, as you can see, then the mercantile."

"They always sing like that?" asked Donnelly, as they got closer to the church. "Sounds like a hundred of 'em at least, maybe more."

"Most likely twenty or thirty at most," said Moriarty. "Just enthusiastic singers is all. They'll be at it quite awhile yet. Seems like every week the singin' goes longer."

When they got as far as Joseph Bean's barber shop, Donnelly noticed that two of the horses out front of it weren't tied up to anything. He didn't need to be too observant, for unlike all the others, these two horses were facing the street rather than the building. It seemed almost like they were watching what was going on, and looking for the people to come out from the church.

"Lookee here," Donnelly said. "Two horses, available free for whoever wants 'em. Fine horses, too. I'll be takin' the gray one when we leave, you can have the other."

"I don't think that's a real good idea," said Moriarty. "They're Wally Davis's horses. The gray one killed a man some time back. Plumb loco, that horse. You don't wanna go anywhere near *him*, not if you value your life. "

"You're a dang liar, Morrison," Donnelly said, stopping to look at the horse — although keeping his distance just in case. "What's he doin' loose then? Most especially if he's a killer!"

"Wally Davis is well liked and respected around here. Gets away with a lot. These horses are trained to stay where he leaves 'em. But I ain't no liar — the horse killed a man. Horace Black, he was called."

"Well, I don't believe you. But then, I don't much like how he's lookin' at me anyways," said Donnelly. "Untrustworthy's my guess — I reckon I'll leave him. Let's get a move on, I don't wish to be seen if I can help it."

The two men walked on further up the street to where the bank stood right next to the new jailhouse, with Roy Black's new saddlery and livery right across from it. Donnelly looked all around the building, checked all the angles where someone might hide to shoot from, and quickly satisfied himself that, if the Sheriff was indeed out of town on some wild goose chase, the bank was a prime target to be sure.

"Might's well slow the Sheriff down a bit too," he said to Moriarty, as the men walked back down the street toward where everyone was still singing in the church. "Which one's his horse?"

"That black one there, why?" said Moriarty, nodding to a horse who was tied to the hitching rail out front of the saloon.

"Figured as much, it's a fine horse," the gunman said. "Faster than any o' these others, except maybe the gray. But I'd say it'd be a close race."

He was half right, Moriarty thought, although he could not have known the gray had won the Billings Cup. Still, it was true, the Sheriff's horse would have been the next-fastest horse in town. "You can't do nothin' to it," said Moriarty. "Everyone'll hear, even over the singin', I'd reckon."

Donnelly looked at Moriarty like he was a fool. "I'll be takin' it with me. I'll hide it away at your place, and use it when we's robbin' the bank. Too slow, that one I bought in Billings. Besides, it'll help slow down the Sheriff when he finally comes after us — that bein' if he's still alive, o' course. Big chance he won't be. And if'n he ain't, he don't need a horse anyways, does he?" And a wicked smile licked across the man's face as he thought of how much he enjoyed killing Sheriffs.

It was too late to argue. Donnelly was already untying the Sheriff's horse. Moriarty was angrier than a bear who just took a bullet in the behind, and was dead afraid someone would come out of the church now and see him with the horse thief. He scurried on ahead, quick as he could, almost walking right into Slowpoke in his hurry, and made for the far corner of the barber shop to hide if he had to. Even in a forgiving place like Come-By-Chance, no one took kindly to horse-thieves, and stealing the Sheriff's own horse was a sure way to get fifteen years.

But just as Moriarty reached the safety of the corner of Joseph Bean's, about fifteen yards ahead of where Donnelly was with the black horse, he heard a small sound. With his heart jumping up in his chest, he wheeled around, just in time to see a small boy reach the bottom of the church steps, wipe his hands on his shirt, look straight across the road to where Slowpoke stood watching, and say, *"Horsie!"*

50

It wasn't that Willie didn't like the singing.

He did.

It was just that he liked horses more.

He had missed Roy and horses so much, having been not allowed near either for a week now, and the moment he had noticed that Coral had taken her eye off him — standing up as they all were, and all engrossed in her singing as she was — he had crawled the short distance past her feet.

The church doors were open just a little, so as to let a breeze through, and Willie shot out through them faster than a bull out a gate.

At the top step, the child stopped a moment and looked around. He did not see his new Pa — Roy had been down the front row of the church, hidden from the youngster's view the whole time — but what he did see was horses, and no shortage of them. And one of them stood out, of course, from the rest — his friend Slowpoke, that huge gentle gray horse he'd been learning to ride on.

The boy made his way down the stairs, checked behind him, and found he had not yet been followed. As he began to cross the street to visit with Slowpoke, another horse, a black one off to his right, began to move slowly toward him. And with that horse was a man.

"*Horsie!*" he said to the man, and kept moving toward Slowpoke.

Dan Donnelly stopped in his tracks. His gaze went from the child to the church doors and back again. He was a horse thief, sure to be caught red-handed any moment. In his haste to keep up his bad reputation, and to show Moriarty he was not afraid of anything, his recklessness had gotten the better of him. He kept hold of the horse's reins with his left hand — he would need to keep the horse between himself and whichever man was to come out those doors — and his right hand went straight to his gun, the coldness of it in his palm making him feel better right away.

He had already decided. There was *nothing* he would not do to get out of this situation.

The child was still moving, had half crossed the road now, still heading toward the gray horse. Moriarty was nowhere to be seen, having disappeared to save his own skin.

"*Willie! Stop!*" came a woman's voice from the top of the church stairs.

The child froze in his tracks in the middle of the street, and another woman arrived, almost right on the heels of the first.

The singing was still going strong as the second woman — recognizing her husband's horse as the one being led away — called, *"Horse thief!"* As she said it, Opal Johnson reached for a gun that wasn't there — for she had taken it off to attend church.

"Hands up, ladies, and don't make a sound," Donnelly said in a low voice, pointing the gun at them from behind the black horse.

As desperate as they were, there was nothing either Coral or Opal could do. The man was just five yards from Willie, and the boy was in the middle of the road, not moving, just looking from Coral to the man, then back to Coral again. The women put their hands in the air, just as Donnelly had told them.

That was when James Moriarty played his hand. He had thought fast as always, known he was likely to be dragged into all this, end up in jail if he was lucky, or in the ground if he wasn't. He saw one chance to turn things around, and he took it.

James Moriarty poked his gun around the corner of Joseph Bean's barber shop, his head out just far enough for one eye to look down the gunsight at Donnelly. And he tried not to shake as he called, "Drop the gun, Mister!"

Dan Donnelly was a gunfighter, and used to fast thinking in such situations. What he saw was a triangle — he himself at one point of it, the ladies at the second, and the double-crosser he'd known as Morrison at the third. And in the middle of it all, a child. If he fired the gun and alerted those inside the church, he had no hope of getting away, not even on this fast horse, for he did not yet know much of the area.

He saw it right away. His only chance was the child.

Dan Donnelly played the one good card he had left. "Drop the gun, Morrison," he said, pointing his own six-shooter at the child. "Or the kid gets the first bullet, and you get the second!"

51

If Coral could have screamed then, she would have. Her mouth opened up wide to do it, but luckily, nothing came out.

The man had his gun pointed at Willie. Her dear little boy in the sights of a gun — and nothing in Coral's life had ever been any more real.

Opal was used to bad situations, and as always, was thinking quite clearly. That much, at least, she had learned from her father. Quietly, calmly, without any movement, she spoke swiftly to James Moriarty. "James. Please. Throw the gun down where he can see it."

Moriarty did as he was told. He was only ten or twelve yards from Donnelly, but his hands were shaking like leaves in a windstorm in Fall, and he could not have shot the side of a barn, even at that distance. He jumped backwards out of sight, throwing the gun forward into the street as he did so, and ran off to find somewhere to hide.

"Stay quiet, Coral," said Opal, "and we'll all get out of this yet."

The singers were nearing the end of their hymn, and Opal knew she needed to get the gunman to leave before she and Coral were missed. "Take the horse, Mister, and ride out of here. I give you my word, we won't raise the alarm. Go!"

"Oh, I'll go alright. And I believe you, lady," the man said. "Because I'll be taking along some insurance."

It all happened so fast then, but each second felt like a lifetime, the whole thing all burned into Coral's memory for the rest of her days.

The singing stopped, giving way to a deafening stillness. The man waved his gun hand about, first at Coral and Opal, then at Willie once more. His eyes went wide as he dropped the reins of the horse, and he moved toward Willie like lightning.

Coral's mouth opened to scream, but once again nothing came out. Willie smiled right at her and said, *"Horsie."*

The man's hand was reaching for Willie, he took his second step and almost his third — when the fastest thing Coral had ever seen, a ruinous dark shadow sent directly from God, flashed into view bent on destruction. And before that reaching hand of violence could get to Willie, in a wild and brutal and calamitous act of annihilation, Slowpoke reared up on his great hind legs, smashing and crashing and pounding his deadly front hooves down upon the man who had dared to threaten a child — and continued to trample the gunman till he was quite dead.

52

In the middle of it all, a shot had been fired.

Coral and Opal were frozen in place, transfixed by the sight of the great gray horse trampling the evil man underfoot.

At the sounds of the violence, people had tried to pour out of the church all at once. Of the men who might have been quickest to act, only Ben Wilkinson had gotten out fast enough to catch the tail end of what had happened. But even before he had time to notice the child, still standing not far from the broken body that lay in the street, Slowpoke, that mostly gentle animal, fleet of foot and pure of heart, finest horse in the Montana Territory, turned away from the man he had killed, and stepped toward Willie Black.

Coral could not speak or breathe. Even Opal did not make a sound, unsure what to do as she stood there. Ben Wilkinson saw the child only when the horse lowered his head and pushed — and Slowpoke, that awful and violent killer of two men, gently nudged Willie in the back, setting the child in motion toward his mother, and did so two more times to keep the boy moving across the street.

Opal helped Coral down the stairs, holding her shaking friend's arm for support, then as Willie jumped up into Coral's arms, the tears began to flow. The first of the tears were from Coral, then the next came from Opal, hers being half from joy and half from the shock of what she had just seen.

Soon there were other tears too, for Roy Black had managed to push his way through the crowd, and, forgetting what he was *supposed to do,* he did exactly what the love in his heart told him to. Roy threw his strong arms around his wife and son, cried along with them, and praised the Lord for making them safe.

"Oh, Roy," cried Coral, "I'm not so sure it was only the Lord, not this time."

"Whatever do you mean, Coral?" Roy said with a most perplexed and grateful look on his face. Perplexed because he still didn't know what had happened, grateful because there had been a shot fired, a man was clearly dead, and his wife and son were quite safe.

Then Willie said, *"Horsie, Pa. Horsie."*

Roy's eyes came alive with love for the boy. He smiled at Willie and ran a hand through his hair, but the hand came out sticky with blood.

There was a lot of confusion, what with everyone milling about, some asking what happened, some telling. Others were telling what they guessed, and still others were telling what they thought they had heard others guess.

In the midst of it all, Roy held his sticky red-smeared hand up in front of his eyes and simply said, "Blood."

Coral's heart just about broke right out of her chest with fear for her son — but Wally Davis, who had finally pushed his way through all the onlookers, and was examining his horse, said, "Don't worry, Coral and Roy. It's just ol' Slowpoke's blood, somehow been dripped on the boy. Poor ol' fella got himself shot in the ruckus somehow."

53

In the end, Slowpoke was fine. It had been a near thing, Dan Donnelly's final act being to get a shot off at the great horse's head. It had gone through the gristle at the base of his ear, leaving him with one ear that never quite sat perfect for the rest of his days. But as Wally said, "A few scars only makes us old fellas even more better lookin' to the ladies anyways. Who woulda thunk it — that he coulda got any more alluring, attractive and pleasingly pulchritudinous than he already was?"

"This is no time for big words, Wallace Erasmus Davis, you fractious old fool!" cried Kate, for she had finally worked out what had happened, close enough. "Somebody could have been killed."

"Somebody was," said Sheriff Johnson, "and I'll be needing to gather up all the facts and the evidence."

By the time all the facts and evidence had been worked out, the sequence of events seemed clear enough.

This horse-thief had met James Moriarty the night

before in Billings, and told him he was headed to the gold diggings near Come-By-Chance. So Moriarty — who had been down South to visit with his dying father — had allowed Donnelly to ride with him, trying to be neighborly. Moriarty reported that the man had been mostly unpleasant, and that, before their arrival at the town, Moriarty had bid him goodbye, then pretended to ride off to his home. He had then doubled back to check on what the man might be up to, and sure enough, found Donnelly's horse tied up two-hundred yards south of the town. Moriarty had followed on foot, then jumped out to save Opal and Coral, but had to put his gun down when Opal requested it — "...after all, the child was in mortal danger."

And so, James Moriarty, with his story all straight, was not only free and clear of all charges, but found himself redeemed in the eyes of the town. He'd had one small piece of explaining to do, when Opal asked why Donnelly had called him Morrison. But his explanation, of having given the man a false name because he seemed untrustworthy, was taken by the Sheriff as being fair enough. And even Opal, who had never trusted Moriarty, could not deny what she had seen — which was that James had done all he could have to save them.

They buried Donnelly in a part of the boneyard away

from everyone else. Some of the townsfolk were against him being buried there at all, but Preacher Coy insisted, and no one was about to argue any further.

Moriarty went home with the best reputation he'd ever yet had in his life, as well as a bottle of Toby Wilkinson's best whiskey, along with everyone's thanks for trying to save the child and the women.

It soon became generally known that, indeed, it had been Slowpoke who had saved Willie from being stolen along with the Sheriff's horse. Most everyone agreed then, that even if he had not won the Billings Cup, he would still be the finest horse in the Territory — but the two things put together most likely made him the best in all the land, or most likely even the world.

Max Milligan announced his intention to write a song in honor of the horse, and set off home to do so, his fiddle being heard to be busy for the next several hours.

And Gilbert's wife, Emmy-Lou, reminded everyone that, "I *did* vote for wonderful Slow-Pokey-Wokey when we held the election for Mayor, and I *might* even do so again the next time we vote, although, in fact, he really did only rescue *one small child,* whereas my Gilbie-Wil-bie rescued a whole church-full of Come-By-Chance folk when that *nasty* Slim Jim tried to burn us all down, but then again, Gilbie did punch my daddy very hard on his jaw, and now that I think of it—"

It was at that point that Bert Heart took a brightly painted spinning top from his pocket and said, "Watch this, Emmy-Lou." He then proceeded to give it a strong spin on the bottom step of the church, the result of which was that Emmy-Lou went completely quiet for a full thirty seconds as she watched it. Thing was, it worked again each time he did so, so fascinated was she by the way the colorfully striped top could spin.

Gilbert was last heard trying to buy the thing from Bert, jokingly offering him a thousand dollars for it — or perhaps it was no joke at all.

The best thing that happened though — and on this the whole town all agreed — was that Roy and Coral and Willie Black all went home together, the adults hand in hand, the child up on Roy's shoulders, a family united once more.

54

THINGS CHANGED MORE EASILY AFTER ALL THAT.

Not all at once, of course — even though Coral had been through some bad things before, the sight of the man being trampled took some time getting over. And seeing Willie in the sights of a gun took even longer. But after all that had happened, Coral found herself listening to the *small voice* a whole lot more than she used to.

She saw right away that Roy had been right about the horse — but he never held it against her, no matter what else was ever said through their lives. He knew she'd had no way of understanding it, at least not until Slowpoke saved Willie's life, just the same as he'd saved Wally's life once before.

It wasn't just the three of them — Roy, Coral and Willie — that made up their family though. From that day on, Coral never doubted that Wally and Kate had only the finest of intentions, and the older couple were greatly honored when Coral asked their permission for Willie to call them Grandpa and Gran.

None of them pushed for it, knowing it was for the best to leave Coral to decide — but after only a few days, Coral requested that Willie be allowed to resume his riding lessons on Slowpoke. Only this time, she wanted to be there to watch, at least for the first little while.

The boy was happier than a baby bird in a water-trough, and the blissful look on his handsome young face just about had everyone's hearts bursting with joy.

Coral watched the first lesson with her eyes half closed and half open — she was a little nervous, true, but after all, she had seen what the horse had done to that man. Still, she knew that the man had deserved it.

In the end, as soon as the first lesson was over, Coral came right out and asked Wally if he might look out for a pony that Willie could have for his own. "A small, quiet, old one perhaps," was how she put it. And Wally told her it was funny she should ask, for he had bought such an animal just a few days before, and had already commenced its training — so if things went well, it might be ready for the boy in just another month or two.

In truth, the pony was not nearly so quiet or old as Wally had made out. In the years to come, that boy and that pony were to be seen having the best of times all around Come-By-Chance, and sometimes even further afield — but still, the bond between Willie and Slow-poke was just as strong too, and if the gray horse was to outlive ol' Wally, everyone knew just whose horse he would become.

He was not left wanting for brothers and sisters either, young Willie Black. After himself came four others, the last of which was named Kate, and sure enough, the child knew lots of big words before long, and had quite the fiery temper, at least when it was called for.

The child before that had been named Wally, and everyone had laughed fit to bust when he was born with a completely bald head, and it took a good year before he got much hair at all.

The one previous to that had been called Maggie, after Roy's dear Ma, and she turned out to be a most gentle soul — except when she rode in the Come-By-Chance rodeo, which she very nearly won every prize at.

But the very first child Coral gave birth to in Come-By-Chance, she insisted on naming Vernon — for without the ultimate sacrifice that Verna, her first mother-in-law, had paid, none of them would have had the chance at happiness she had given them. And Vernon, he turned out to be not just a brother, but the greatest friend Willie ever had, the pair of them having such adventures as would even have made Wally Davis's hair stand on end, that being if he'd had any hair, which he didn't.

As for Coral herself, she had such a friend too. She and Opal stuck by each other through thick and thin.

In fact, whenever Beryl Waters came to visit, which was regular as clockwork, twice a year — Willie called her Gramma B for the rest of her days — she would always say they were like an old married couple, the way they bickered and laughed and finished each other's sentences all the time.

As it turned out, it was just as well they had each other too, for not everything in their future would be rosy. As good as things seemed right now, with Willie learning to ride, and Coral and Roy back to sharing their bed with each other at night, they knew nothing of what was on its way. Opal's father was not the sort of man to give up — the bank would soon be opening, and wherever there's money and men who'd rather steal it than earn it, there's about to be a whole mess of trouble. Not to mention, the man was still out for revenge.

But for now, the town of Come-By-Chance was quiet and safe, and Willie Black lay in his bed, a smile spreading out across his face, for as always, he was dreaming of horses.

THE END

Thank You for Reading

I hope you enjoyed reading Coral's story as much as I enjoyed writing it.

To be first to know when other books in the series are released, please come to my webpage at
julietjamesbooks.wordpress.com
and sign up for my newsletter.

Or just come to the webpage to say *Hi.*
I love hearing from readers, and although it might take me a day or two, I can promise I'll always reply.

I hope you'll come back to Come-By-Chance soon, to catch up with the whole gang, and whoever the next new bride is. Whoever she is, it won't be easy for her either — but that's part of what makes life worthwhile.

Books by Juliet James

COME-BY-CHANCE BRIDES OF 1884 SERIES

1 - Ruby
2 - Emily
3 - Violet
4 - Kate
5 - Rose
6 - Emmy-Lou

COME-BY-CHANCE BRIDES OF 1885 SERIES

1 - Opal
2 - Coral
Future Releases:
3 - Ava & Ina
4 - Pearl
5 - Tina
6 - Jane

Recommended Reading

Books by Annie Lane

Seasons Mail Order Bride Series

1 - Charlotte's Summer
2 - Falling for Beth
3 - Alice in Winterland
4 - Spring Belle

Seasons Sons & Daughters Mail Order Bride Series

1 - Madeline's Match
2 - Hannah's Hope
Future Releases:
3 - Sarah's Choice
4 - Stella's Fella

Books by Tara Sharp & Juliet James

Sᴘɪʀɪᴛ ᴏғ Gᴏᴅ Lᴏᴠᴇ Sᴛᴏʀɪᴇs

1 - How Sweet the Sound
2 - Little White Lies
3 - Sarah's Dream

Made in the USA
San Bernardino, CA
14 May 2017